THE FOURTH LEVEL

FIRESTORM

BOOK NINE

NICHOLAS HUNTLEY

BERWICK-NORTHUMBRIA NATIONAL PARK

"But no one will ask us whether we do or do not will it, when the spiritual strength of the West fails and the joints of the world no longer hold, when this moribund semblance of culture caves in and lets it suffocate in madness. Whether this will happen depends alone on whether or not we, as a historical-spiritual people, still and once again will ourselves."

– Martin Heidegger

Act 1, Scene 1

The glare of the rising sun poked through the pine-bearing branches in the boreal forest around. The tops of the trees reached upwards to the clear blue sky above. The thick coniferous trees of the forest whose trunks were wide and old, rooted into the earth with firm roots that sometimes protruded outwards and in around the ground. The ground of which was not consistent in the level of its surface, but dynamic in its slopes and straights, nor was its composition made entirely of dirt, but of moss and lichen, and pebbles and rocks throughout. The youthful soil was a dark shade of brown and almost as dry as a desert's sands.

A red squirrel dashed across a set of branches with pines waving upwards and downwards in the wind. The sound of birds chirping could be heard throughout, woodpeckers gnawing at the trunks of trees, and the flow of water not too far. Nearby, there was a steady stream of water flowing over and around the rocks of a creek, and was absolutely clear and transparent. The water formed ripples at its landings, flowing downwards in smaller bodies before fastening in speed the more rocks that presented in the form of obstacles, creating whitewater that sprayed around and cascaded downwards to the larger body of water below.

The whole of the creek stretched along for miles, forming a larger lake at the end, but in the opposite direction, it ran upwards along a smooth hill with trees and shrubs at its side as well as tall grass. From above, the stream of water was small and insignificant to the image of the entire forest as a whole whose tall trees stretched for miles and miles in either direction with the odd blemish of mounds of rocks, clearings of land, or ditches of ponds and lakes along the landscape. The sun peaked over the horizon and painted the land in a warm summer light that brought a richer color to the flora throughout.

Below, travelling with a small escort of three mercenaries, Diana and Tristan crossed the shallow waters of a calm stream to the reach the other side of the dense forest they were surrounded by on their hike. Diana's hair, tied in a ponytail, was more noticeably brown than black in the light of the sun. Her hair was also a fair length, but had not grown as nearly as much as Tristan's whose hair hadn't been cut in the last two months. Tristan's red-blonde hair was almost wavy and thick, pulling to the back of his neck and behind his ears. He wore a grey short-sleeved shirt that showed his self-earned figure and firm arms. He held on to his black backpack by the straps, flexing his biceps. His skin was tanned and golden arm hair obscure. He also wore beige shorts and brown hiking boots. In the span of two months, Tristan had grown an extra inch and was almost six feet and two inches tall compared to last summer when he was two inches less.

Diana was in a healthy state as well and held a quaint smile. Her skin was not tanned, but as fair as always and brighter in the light of the summer sky. Her blue eyes were focused on the space ahead of her and like Tristan, she held onto the straps of her backpack as she crossed the waters in her own hiking boots. The denim shorts she wore were shorter than Tristan's, exposing her hairless legs and smooth skin, reaching almost halfway up her thighs. She wore a white shirt as well as an open red-black flannel shirt that was almost too large for her as it belonged to Tristan. Diana was the same height as she was around this time last year.

The couple were accompanied by the Protection Squad who were dressed in their camouflage smocks with belts around the waist, suspenders loaded with munitions, and backpacks on their backs. They also wore field caps, jackets beneath the smocks, and trousers in a pixelated greenish-grey as opposed to the standard urban black. Each of them were armed with semi-automatic rifles and nothing more but some knives. Lukas 'Sceafa' Scaravetti, the senior member of the team in charge of the protection of the children with 'Elegast,' the Dutchman, and 'Lacplesis,' the Latvian, led the children through the water and to the other side where there were bushes and shrubs at the base of a small hill leading back into the forest.

The group continued their hike under shade, venturing forward and deeper inward where there was tall grass at their feet. Diana and Tristan stayed close together, walking side by side in silence as Lukas continued to lead and the other two walked from behind. All of them walked in a calm pace through the forest, continuing along and past some tall trees whose trunks were skinnier than others they had seen. The trees had a grey bark over their trunks, were naked for approximately half of their length with thin branches holding pines on the other half. These pine trees were spread out around them.

The smooth walk before them soon turned into a slope as they continued along with a greater density of shrubbery at their sides.

"How much longer do we have to walk?" Tristan questioned. "We've been at it for almost an hour."

"Not much longer," Lukas responded in a rich Lombardy accent, looking at his watch. "The meeting point is not too far from here. Be a little patient, Tristan."

"We've been through longer hikes in the Russian and Arctic cold," Diana replied to Tristan. "What's the hurry?"

"We haven't seen him in almost two months," Tristan responded. "I'm anxious."

"Are you sure you're not just out of shape?" Diana teased.

Tristan looked at her with a frown and replied, "I love being out here, but I don't understand why he couldn't have just met us in London instead of keeping us in anticipation for a whole week more."

"He said he was busy…" Diana replied, stopping Tristan as they walked by taking his hand. "Judith's death had a real effect on him…. He needed time to be alone, so don't act upset or bitter, especially when we see him. The last thing you need to do to him is to make him feel guilty for abandoning us."

"He didn't abandon us…" Tristan corrected. "I'm not mad."

Diana looked at him and then over to Lukas as he stopped and looked to them.

"I'm sorry, but I thought you were in a hurry," Lukas remarked to them.

"Sorry," Diana apologized to him, walking forward. "We are."

The grass at their feet began to thin out and be replaced by a coarse dirt with stones protruding from the earth. On their left, Tristan could see some purple flowers with long stems. They were lavenders.

Tristan looked behind him and could see that they had ventured a fair distance upwards and were at least fifty meters above the height of the river. The steepness of the hillside pushed them to follow a natural path along the slope that gradually led them upwards some more meters. The path continued along parallel to the hill and then turned the opposite direction to continue.

Eventually, they reached the top of the path and came out of the forest. The view from the top of the hill they had climbed gave them a broad and extensive view of coniferous trees for miles around them as well as the sight of a large lake in the horizon with a view of further coniferous trees atop of a cliff on the other side. Ahead of them, further along the edge of the hill, they saw before them someone who they hadn't seen in a long time.

Charlemagne stood at the edge of the hill with a foot atop of a rock and his face looking forward towards the rest of the forest below. The sun shined down hard on them and forced Charlemagne to shield his eyes with his right hand. He wasn't dressed in his typical suit, but was dressed for the occasion with hiking boots and beige socks pulled up over his legs. He wore dark beige shorts with a black belt, a navy blue and white flannel shirt, buttoned up and tucked into his shorts, and an Australian-style bush hat that matched his shorts. He also had a large backpack behind him and a confident expression over his face. His hair was much as it was when they last saw him, trimmed to be as it usually was, and his moustache likewise.

Behind him was Miklos, standing in the shade of a tree and before a path that went back into the forest. He was with Igor who was sat on a fallen log. Each of them wore sunglasses over his eyes and was dressed in the same attire as the others, but Miklos with his sleeves rolled up. Miklos' hair also appeared to have grown and not been trimmed since they had seen him in France, recovering from his injuries sustained by the Mysterious Stranger none of them had seen since the incident in France.

Lukas stopped before him and the kids caught up to stand next to him as they looked at Charlemagne. Charlemagne looked back at them and retracted his foot from the rock to face them. His confident-serious expression turned to a confident smile as he looked at the kids.

"Charles," Diana greeted, rushing towards him and hugging him.

"It's so good to see you Diana," Charlemagne expressed in his same East Anglian accent. "I've missed you both so much."

Tristan walked forward and stood by Diana as the two continued to hug for an extra couple of seconds before Charlemagne let go and faced Tristan. Charlemagne looked to him with a serious face.

"Hello, Tristan," Charlemagne greeted, offering his hand.

Tristan took his hand to shake and then was pulled in for a hug. Charlemagne patted Tristan's back and then the two separated.

"Thank you, Luka, for bringing my children to me in one piece," Charlemagne regarded, looking over to him. "There wasn't any trouble with customs? No trouble elsewhere on your way here?"

"No, sir," Lukas replied. "Mr. Heavner saw to it that we would not have any issues."

"Good," Charlemagne responded, looking at the kids and then extending his arm towards the view of the forest. "Children, I would like to welcome you to the British Isles. Specifically, I would like to welcome you to Berwick-Northumbria National Park – Britain's largest national park, so large that it encompasses both England and Scotland as somewhere within this forest, one can cross into either or. We are, of course, in England, but if all goes according to plan, then I hope to take you from where we are now in Northumbria and go upwards towards Berwick in the Scotland."

"I didn't realize England had any national parks to begin with until we got here yesterday," Tristan remarked, looking out to the view and crossing his arms. "It's beautiful."

"Yes, a reminder of how the island once was," Charlemagne replied, looking to Diana and then Tristan. "A homeland for the proud British people."

Diana looked to Charlemagne and then out to the view. The two continued to look forward. Tristan turned around and looked over to Miklos. Diana noticed that they were no longer looking at the view and instead over to Miklos. Charlemagne also noticed and looked to his old friend.

"It's good to see you again too," Tristan said to him.

"Likewise," Miklos replied in a dull tone through his Hungarian accent.

"How are you?" Tristan asked.

"I'm alive," Miklos responded, shrugging. "I've had worse calls in the past."

Tristan smiled at him and shook his head.

"How stoic," Tristan remarked.

"Yes, we're all very impressed with you, Miko," Charlemagne replied to him, "but you had me in quite a fright regardless."

"You worry too much, Charles," Miklos suggested.

"Anyways," Charlemagne responded, looking to the kids. "Let's not waste away at the time in the day – we've got a couple of miles to go before we reach a space I spent quite a bit of time selecting for us. It'll be a fine campground for us – we have an entire summer ahead of us of camping and wilderness, after all."

Act 1, Scene 2

Charlemagne led the group downhill and through the forest a couple of miles until they reached a rocky terrain that looked outwards towards a lake. The beach ahead of them consisted entirely of stones and included a large boulder leading upwards to a clearing of rocks and dirt before some more rocks that led up to a clearing of porous dirt and grass where they had arrived to. The area was surrounded by skinnier trunked trees than the pine trees in the forest as these were entirely covered with branches of pines. They were fir trees. The lake was calm and reflected only the evergreen trees around them and the light blue sky above. Its water was absolutely clear that the rocks within the depths of the lake could be seen. Behind the lake was a small mountain. Beyond the rocky beach, the rest of the rim of the lake consisted of grass and fir trees. There were a minor amount of bushes around them.

"Well, what do you think?" Charlemagne questioned. "I found this little space yesterday and thought it would be a perfect space to set up camp. We can set up the tents right here as it's not too near the water and in an open space, and we can have the fire below near the beach as there is little risk of anything spreading. Beyond these bushes, we can set up a small bathroom."

"You've really thought through this," Tristan remarked. "It is nice."

"I thought so," Charlemagne replied, smiling. "Now come on. We've got lots of setting up to do. We better start with a fire. Diana and Tristan, can you go back into the woods and fetch some tinder, kindling and fuel? I'll get a pit started by the beach so we can have some lunch starting to cook."

"Sure," Tristan replied, looking to Diana.

"For tinder, we'll need either some bark or…"

"I know what to look for," Tristan responded. "Don't worry, this isn't my first time camping in the great outdoors. Come on," he added to Diana, walking off with her.

Charlemagne looked to Tristan with a shrewd smile and then to the mercenaries.

"Lukas, make sure they don't get lost," Charlemagne requested before looking to Miklos. "Help me move some stones."

Diana and Tristan went into the forest where they started to look for the desired items.

"So, what are we looking for?" Diana asked Tristan.

"Something light to start a fire, and then something a little bigger to kindle the fire, and then something bigger to keep the fire burning," Tristan explained. "If we rushed to the fuelwood, we risk putting the entire fire out, so we need to gradually build up what we feed. Ideally, kindling can be just some sticks, but the fuelwood will need to be actual logs."

"Okay…" Diana replied, looking around. "What about moss for tinder?"

"Yeah, that can work too, but make sure it's not wet or anything," Tristan responded, taking out his hatchet from his backpack to shave some bark off of some trees.

Diana picked up some moss and then some grass. Tristan shaved off a decent layer off of a fallen log and then passed it to Diana. Meanwhile, she looked around and picked up some loose sticks that had fallen around. Once Tristan was finished shaving enough bark for them, he walked off to join with her near where there were some dead trees on the ground. Tristan took his axe and started to hack at the log, severing it from its roots and limiting its size for him to drag back to the camp site.

"I think I have enough tinder and kindling," Diana said, walking over to Tristan as he hacked at a log. "I'm going back to the camp."

"Sure," Tristan replied, "I'll be right behind you."

Tristan put his hatchet away and then picked up the two logs he had collected. Each of them were approximately less than half a foot thick in diameter. He dragged them from where he had found them and walked a short distance back to the camp and down towards the top of the beachhead where Charlemagne was arranging large rocks in a U-formation. Diana set down her collection and Tristan left the logs nearby.

"Thank you," Charlemagne said, on his knees and finishing the formation. "Bring me some of that grass over here."

Diana lowered her backpack and then got down on her knees to give Charlemagne some of the grass. Charlemagne placed the grass at the bottom of the U-formation and then took some bark with it.

"How are you going to light the fire?" Tristan questioned. "Flint and steel? Magnifying glass?"

"Matches," Charlemagne simply replied, producing some matches from his backpack in a plastic sandwich bag. "I'm not going to waste my time with some convoluted means to start a fire – we're recreationally camping, not a part of some sort of survival simulation."

Tristan held a frown over his face and watched as Charlemagne simply lit a match and then dropped it into the tinder. The grass and bark caught on fire, which allowed Charlemagne to take some branches and snap them into smaller pieces. Diana and Tristan helped him feed the fire before looking to the large log that Tristan had brought. Charlemagne took his own hatchet from his backpack and went over to the logs.

"We'll need these in smaller pieces," Charlemagne said. "Help me with the other log."

Tristan took his hatchet from his backpack and helped Charlemagne reduce the logs into smaller pieces. Once Charlemagne had two logs approximately less than a foot in length, he lowered them atop of the kindling and tinder, dimming the fire slightly, but it continued to burn and eventually consumed the log to produce a brighter and larger flame.

"There we are," Charlemagne remarked, taking out a rectangular grate from his backpack. "Something not too large, but large enough that we can boil water and cook our meals."

Charlemagne placed the grate over the fire and proceeded to retrieve some pots and pans from his backpack, setting them over the grate.

"What do you kids fancy for lunch?" Charlemagne questioned.

"Do we have much of a choice?" Tristan replied.

"I'm afraid not," Charlemagne answered. "All I have is a bit of meat I bought from the stores before we arrived to the forest and some rice, so that'll have to be it. A bit of curry sauce, and that'll be our lunch. For supper, I hope we can do a bit of fishing if we have time. If not, we do have various ration packs and such, but there's no fun in that of course."

Charlemagne stood up with a large pot and filled it with water from the lake. He then returned to his fire and set it atop of the grill and poured some uncooked rice he had into the pot. Once the rice was starting off, he retrieved a large bag of meat from his backpack and fetched a large knife to begin cutting it up.

"Is that enough for the seven of us?" Diana questioned.

"I'm only cooking for the three of us," Charlemagne replied. "Miklos and his peers would rather cook their own food than have me cook for them."

Tristan looked over to the mercs as they had finished setting up their tents on the outskirts of the campsite.

"How about instead of sitting there, the two of you begin to set up your tents," Charlemagne suggested. "No sense in watching me cook – lunch will be a while until it's ready. I'll join you in a minute or two."

"Sure," Tristan replied, standing up and looking to Diana. "Come on."

Diana stood up and went up the plateau to where Charlemagne wanted them to set up their tents. Tristan retrieved their tent packs from both of their backpacks and then joined her. The mercenaries had set up their tents not too far from where they would place theirs, but appeared to have established all four of theirs in a sort of perimeter at the mouth of the camp site, spread apart from one another.

"Thank you," Diana said, taking her tent pack into her hand and taking out what was inside.

Diana dumped the components on the ground before her to Tristan's annoyance. He threw his pack on the ground and then looked at Diana.

"Not quite like the tents we had in Russia," Tristan said. "Let me help you build yours."

"No, let me do it," Diana remarked. "I'll be fine – I have instructions."

"Are you sure?" Tristan questioned.

"If there's anything Judith taught me, it's to be a little independent," Diana replied. "Just let me try and do it on my own."

"I'm not quite sure she's one to take lessons from," Tristan muttered to himself.

Tristan shrugged and then picked up his pack. He took his tent next to Diana's, on the edge of the plateau facing the lake and took out the first piece, which was a coat. He laid it down and then took out the body of the tent and placed it atop, marking each tab with one another before taking out the poles and assembling them. The poles were thin tubule pieces made of metal that snapped together to form a thin skeleton, or cross that attached to the body of the tent via grommets, or holes at each corner of the tent body and coat. The tubules were connected to one another via an underlying string. Once the frame was set up, the body of the tent attached to the poles via plastic clips. Once the tent was raised up and structurally sound, Tristan placed a rainfly over the body of the tent and aligned the door of the rainfly with the body door. He then attached the rainfly to the poles via the grommets before taking out the stakes.

Each stake went through the grommet and was hammered into the ground. Once Tristan was finished, he unzipped the door of the tent, crawled inside, and sat down to look over to the lake. He then leaned forward and looked over to Diana as she struggled to line the poles right. Tristan sighed and stood up to help her.

"Here," Tristan said, taking the pole. "You've got to connect these two pieces and form a cross, and then you need to place the ends of each pole through these little holes in the corner of the body.

Tristan helped her raise her tent just as he did with his. By the time he was hammering the stakes, Charlemagne walked up from the beach and proceeded to put together his own tent next to them.

"Watch it," Charlemagne warned, pointing to Tristan as he hammered the stake. "Be sure those are at a forty-five degree angle away from the tent."

Tristan did not respond and silently removed the stake to redo them. Once they were finished, he went to his tent and did the same.

"There we are," Charlemagne commended, standing up and bringing his hands to his hips. "We've got the basics, but we'll need to go and dig a hole out for private use and perhaps set up a clothes line for laundry – over there by the beach between those two trees would do nicely. Tristan, take the wire from my backpack and go and set it up with Diana. I'm going to check on our lunch."

"Yes, sir," Tristan replied, going down to the beach with him and Diana.

Charlemagne handed him the wire and the two then set off for the thin trees to wrap the wire around both trunks and form a sharp wireline. Once the wire was set, the couple returned to Charlemagne where he was serving food onto some plates. The meat had blended with the curry sauce was served atop of the white rice. Charlemagne handed a plate to Diana and then Tristan before taking his own plate. He was sure to remove the pots from the grill and leave them on the side. Charlemagne set a clean pot atop of the fire with some water inside to boil. He also added some kindle to the fire before sitting down on the rocks around them to eat.

"I'll have some tea in a bit," Charlemagne said, picking up his plate and looking around. "Well, it's not much, but this is what home will be like at least for the weekend. If there's anything you feel we should add, we can get to it today."

"How about some seats so we don't have to sit on the ground?" Tristan questioned, adjusting himself into the rocks.

Charlemagne nodded as he handed each of them some forks and knives.

"Certainly," Charlemagne responded, "perhaps we can find a log or two and can create some hard cushions. We'll finish setting up this camp and keep our activities to a minimum for now – perhaps we can go for another hike later, but tomorrow is when the real work begins, so prepare yourself for that."

Act 1, Scene 3

Later the same night, Charlemagne sat with the kids around the campfire where they were roasting marshmallows and enjoying the solitude of the quiet outdoors. Diana and Tristan sat on the rocks with their backs against a log while Charlemagne sat across from them, atop of a log and writing into a journal. He wore his reading glasses as he wrote with the light of the fire in front of them. The Protection Squad was in their tents and had retired for the night.

"What have you been up to in the last two months?" Tristan asked Charlemagne.

"I told you before I left," Charlemagne responded, continuing to write. "I was on tour with Marcel Maurras and other populist figures, giving speeches throughout Europe on the importance of conserving and protecting European people and culture. Why?"

"Tell us more – you can't simplify the last two months away from us to a mere sentence," Tristan argued. "I want to know each and every place you went to, the people you were with, and more."

Charlemagne stopped writing in his journal and looked over to Tristan. He took off his glasses and closed his book. He then put both aside next to him on the log and brought his hands together as he looked to the kids.

"Very well," Charlemagne said, "I suppose I owe you a detailed explanation into my activities and experiences in the last two month. After Judith's funeral and when you kids went back to the manor, I spent another couple days in Paris where I met with Mr. Maurras and other officials of his party. I then returned to Orleans with Dr. Dumas, Manon's father, and went to see Jacques again before going to see Manon. The week after,

Mr. Maurras took me to Belgium, the Netherlands, Luxembourg, Germany, and then we travelled northwards to the northern states of Norway, Sweden, and Finland. The status of both Germany and Sweden left a particular impression on me – cities like Malmo, Stockholm, and Frankfurt and Munich were in a rough state. There is an endless violence in Sweden in particular due to migrants, especially in these areas known as 'No-go Zones,' and we spoke about that to our audiences. There were," he sighed, "a lot of protests with our presence and sometimes violence, especially in Germany, but there was also support. My time in Italy was met with a considerable amount of support from the people there – nice people – tired people. People who are tired of the violence…"

Charlemagne took a moment to breath.

"From Italy then, we went into Austria and then Czech Republic into Poland. From Poland we went upwards to the Baltics and then back down through Belarus and Ukraine into Romania and then Hungary. In Hungary, Miklos took me to his home and I met with Tanya and their four-year old son in their hometown. We spent a nice afternoon in Budapest before we went onwards down through Croatia and Serbia, and then into Greece. My time in Eastern Europe was better spent than in the west. I sometimes loathed being in the Netherlands or Germany or Sweden, but from Italy onwards, with possibly the exception of Czechia and Romania, there was a juxtaposed hospitality rather than hostility from the people up until Greece. Our voyage finished in Portugal and Spain – I spoke in Madrid on the Catalan Crisis and then we went to Ireland and finally here. The situation in Dublin and London is horrendous, but you might have seen the state of London when you arrived here…"

"So," Diana remarked, "you're some sort of right-wing populist then. An advocate against anti-immigration and globalism."

"And there's nothing wrong with that," Tristan added before Charlemagne could respond, "but when are you going to talk in the U.S. and Canada? When are you going to run for office? The municipal elections for Allabrese are coming up this autumn – are you going to run for mayor?" he asked.

"I'm not a politician, Tristan," Charlemagne brushed aside. "I'm not going to run for office – not now, not ever. I can't be bothered with the poisons of parliamentarian politics and their appeal to the emotions of people who are so blindsided by the media. I'm disenchanted with democracy and politics, and do not wish to see myself in either."

Charlemagne sighed once more.

"I prefer the homeliness of Allabrese in all honesty and my work with Cabernet Industries. Our brothers in Europe deserve a home like we have but are cut short by the greed of others. For as long as Cabernet Industries is my company, I will be sure that we are a counter-force to the greed of these corporations. I will be sure that we invest in our people to the end."

"How's Manon?" Diana asked. "Is she okay?"

"Manon?" Charlemagne questioned. "Of course she's fine – after the funeral, she returned to Toulouse to finish the semester."

"How come she didn't travel with you?" Tristan questioned. "I thought she would have shared your enthusiasm or have been sure to stick around after what happened. Didn't you two make up?"

Charlemagne groaned and went quiet. He looked to the side and then back to the kids.

"In a manner of speaking, we attempted to repair the divide between us since I made my grave mistake, but there are still bitter feelings that perhaps may never be set aside," Charlemagne responded. "I hurt her more than I had imagined and I don't deserve to be forgiven or with her because of what I did."

"You should still try," Tristan encouraged. "She loves you. You love her. You made a mistake, but you're better together."

"No," Charlemagne denied, shaking his head, "even if it were possible right now, it is too soon for me after Judith. Listen, children, Manon and I are in a better state than we were before we travelled to France – we are in frequent contact, and that is where I would like to remain at the moment."

"Things change," Tristan advised. "I just want you to be happy, Charles."

"Thank you, Tristan," Charlemagne replied, "but I should be encouraging the same from the two of you. I've never meddled into your personal relations and would appreciate it if you dropped this idea of me and Manon being together again."

Diana and Tristan looked at each other.

"Do you know?" Diana questioned, looking back at Charlemagne. "About us?"

"Diana," Tristan scolded.

"What about you?" Charlemagne asked.

"Nothing," Diana deflected.

"About what we've been up to," Tristan instead said. "Diana wants you to ask about us – about what we've been doing."

"Right," Charlemagne responded, clearing his throat, "how selfish of me. Of course, I meant to ask and have been curious. What have the two of you been up to? How's school been? I only know as much as what Lukas and Mavis have told me, so go ahead and tell."

Diana and Tristan looked at each other again. Tristan looked back to Charlemagne and shrugged.

"School's school," Tristan simply said. "There's nothing more to say than that."

"How did your final exams go?" Charlemagne questioned. "Are you set for your final year of high school? Have you been keeping up with your driving lessons?"

"Yes," Tristan responded, "and my exams went fine."

"How about lacrosse? Did your team make it to the finals?" Charlemagne asked.

"No, but that gave me more time to focus on track and field to be honest," Tristan replied. "I didn't make it to any of the finals in that either though."

"And how about you, Diana?" Charlemagne questioned. "How did your final exams go?"

"Okay…" Diana replied, shrugging. "I passed all my classes."

"How has work been?" Charlemagne asked. "Saved many lives?"

"The pool's been quiet, but it's been getting a little busier – they're not too happy that I decided to go on vacation at the busiest time of the year and I was a little decisive on taking a break, but it's okay. We're a little short-handed on lifeguards at the moment."

"Do you like your job?" Charlemagne questioned.

"It's a part-time job," Diana reasoned. "It's given me some interesting experiences, but not what I see myself doing for the rest of my life."

"Of course," Charlemagne replied, looking back to both of the kids. "Anyways, how was your flight from Allabrese? What did you get up to in the last week before we met?"

"We spent almost two days getting used to the time difference in London," Tristan explained. "We went to the Tower of London, London Eye, Westminster Palace, Buckingham Palace, Westminster Abbey, and St. Paul's Cathedral... What else did we do?"

"We went to the National Gallery and that was pretty much else for London because then we went to see the Cliffs of Dover, and then the next day we went to Portsmouth to make our way to Baths. We then passed through Bristol to get to Birmingham where we went to an aquarium and saw some penguins. Then the next day we came to Manchester and saw a soccer game. Finally, we came to Newcastle where we got all the equipment you asked us to bring with us and then we came here early this morning."

"Seems as though you've seen the best of England with the exception of East Anglia where I grew up – you'll have to visit there before you leave," Charlemagne stated. "It's a worthwhile trip."

"We leave? Are you not coming back to Canada with us?" Diana questioned.

"I haven't decided yet," Charlemagne simply responded, "but it is likely."

"Charles, what are we doing here?' Diana then asked. "Of all the places to meet you, why this forest? It seems a little odd. Canada has much larger forests to go camping in, so what are we doing all the way in England?"

"Well, for a start, there are no bears in England which makes the experience a little safer," Charlemagne remarked, "but in all honesty, I wanted you to have an experience in English wilderness – the beauty of the natural forest from the largest national park on the entire British Isles. England as she once was... because now all England and by extension, Britain, is a compartmentalized urban center with national parks acting as nothing more than parks instead of large forests to explore. I wanted you to have that experience, because it's one that might not survive into next century."

Diana did not reply to Charlemagne. Instead, the three of them went quiet and within a minute of that silence, Charlemagne stood up.

"Right, well, I'm glad we could have the time to talk and catch up, but it's time we all went to bed for the night. We have a long day ahead of tomorrow and I don't want either of you to be tired," Charlemagne said, picking up a bucket of water and tossing it into the fire. "Run along now."

Diana picked up a flashlight that was lying next to her and turned it on. She and Tristan then walked back to their tents while Charlemagne scathed the ashes of the fire before going to fetch some more water. Diana unzipped her tent door and looked inside to where her sleeping bag was laying. She then looked to Tristan as she got on her knees to crawl into her tent. He was bent forward and looking to her.

"What the heck is wrong with you?" Tristan questioned in a quiet voice.

"What are you talking about?" Diana replied.

"You almost outed us," Tristan argued, looking at her. "He doesn't know we're together."

"Sorry," Diana responded with a sincere apologetic expression, "I thought he said that he knew about us, but simply never said anything about it because he thought it wasn't his business – I'm tired and misinterpreted his words."

Tristan rolled his eyes and then gave a sigh.

"I'm sorry," Diana said again.

"It's fine," Tristan responded, giving an apologetic smile to her before straightening up. "I'll see you tomorrow."

"Wait," Diana said, turning around to sit down and look at him properly, "I also thought that with Lukas and the others keeping an eye on us for so long that they knew too and told him. I wouldn't put it pass them or even Charles to know."

Tristan looked at her with an anxious face.

"Thanks, I'm sure to sleep in peace now…" Tristan responded.

"If they do know, they don't care," Diana replied, "and why should they? I…"

Tristan looked behind him as he saw Charlemagne approaching. He then looked back to Diana.

"We'll talk about this tomorrow," Tristan said in a rush. "I love you – goodnight."

"Goodnight," Diana replied, watching him off before closing her tent door.

Diana backed up to her sleeping bag and sat down atop.

"Love you too," Diana said, taking a deep sigh.

Act 1, Scene 4

Early next morning, Charlemagne fetched their food from a large sack hanging from a tree. He then took the items over to create a new fire and proceeded to break some eggs to make some breakfast in a pan. He fried some bread with the eggs and around the time that it was ready, he saw Tristan exit from his tent to join him.

"Good morning," Charlemagne greeted in an energetic tone. "Do you mind fetching me some water from the lake? I want to set some to boil to make some instant coffee."

"Sure…" Tristan responded, taking the pot over to the lake and filling it with water.

Tristan returned the pot to Charlemagne who laid it next to the pan with their eggs.

"How do you prefer your eggs?" Charlemagne questioned. "Scrambled or over easy?"

"I'll take mine scrambled," Tristan responded, scratching his head. "Charles, can I ask your opinion on something?"

"Certainly, my dear boy," Charlemagne replied, "whatever is on your mind."

"It's about Diana," Tristan said, "and it's serious."

Tristan took a deep breath. Charlemagne looked to him.

"I think I like her… more than just liking her. I'm attracted to her and want to have a relationship with her…" Tristan expressed. "Is that wrong?"

Charlemagne looked at him and then looked to the side. He looked to the lake and then down their food.

"Do you have reason to believe she likes you too?" Charlemagne questioned.

"Possibly," Tristan responded, "but would it be okay? How would other people see it? Is it a taboo? We're not related, per say, but we're still adopted-siblings, so it is a *little* weird to say the least."

Charlemagne sighed and served the eggs onto a plate. He then handed it to Tristan.

"It's an awkward subject, Tristan," Charlemagne confessed, scratching his head. "The problem I have with it is the matter that the two of you live together in close quarters in the manor… If she doesn't…"

Diana unzipped her tent door and stepped out. The two of them looked over to her. She smiled at them and went down towards them.

"Never mind," Tristan said, looking to Charlemagne. "You're right – it would be weird. Let's pretend like I never said anything ever."

"What's weird?" Diana questioned, sitting down next to him.

"A bad joke I just made," Tristan deflected. "How did you sleep?"

"Not that bad… there's a big difference sleeping in a sleeping bag on the ground and sleeping on one atop of an inflated mattress," Diana remarked. "What's for breakfast?"

"Eggs and bread," Charlemagne replied, looking to Tristan who was looking at Diana. "Tristan, once you're finished your breakfast, I want you and Miklos to go out and do some fishing at the nearby river we passed on our way here. I would help, but I'm going to set out to design some primitive land traps so we can entrap, with some hope, a hare if we're lucky."

"Sure thing," Tristan replied, nodding as she looked back to Charlemagne.

"Can I help?" Diana asked. "I don't mind."

"I have another task for you," Charlemagne said, serving her a plate and handing it to her. "It'll be as important, but right up your alley – it involves reading."

"I do like to read," Diana smiled as she took the plate, looking to Tristan.

Tristan gave an awkward smile and then continued to eat. The family ate their breakfast in more or less silence. Once they were finished, Charlemagne took their plates and set off to wash them in a bucket of soapy water. Meanwhile, Diana left to finish getting ready for the day, leaving Tristan on his own, which he spent away from Charlemagne and instead atop of a boulder, looking out to the lake. Upon Diana's return, he handed him the toothpaste and he left to go wash his own teeth. Diana then went to Charlemagne.

"I'm ready for my task, master," Diana said, standing before him.

"Ah, good," Charlemagne replied, standing up and going to his tent.

Diana waited by the beach and Charlemagne returned with a book.

"Your task is to watch the campfire while I'm off setting a trap, and while you're doing that, I need you to have a look through this," Charlemagne said, handing her the book.

"Did your reading glasses break overnight?" Diana jested.

Charlemagne looked at her and then said, "No, but I want you to familiarize yourself with the basic points of this book, especially the part on identifying plants and berries. I want to take a stab at harvesting what nature has to offer us. Tomorrow, it'll be Tristan's turn to read the book and watch the campfire, and so on..."

"Okay..." Diana replied, looking through the book. "I'll just lie over here on the beach, soak up some sun, and read..."

"Thank you," Charlemagne replied, looking over as Tristan was about to return.

Tristan came to Charlemagne and two began to walk away from the beach up to where Charlemagne had a bag with some fishing poles and other accessories inside. Tristan took the bag and brought it around his shoulder by the strap. He then picked up a circular container next to him.

"Did you keep Diana from helping based on what I said to you?" Tristan questioned.

"Nonsense," Charlemagne responded, "I have no issue with you spending time with Diana – I had just learned what you had told me, and even now, I have no business getting in the way of you two. The last thing I wish to do is to come between your friendship with her."

"Right…" Tristan responded, "… it's just a weird task getting someone to read something."

"It's an important survival book and given the matter that she has never been camping before, it would do her well to familiarize herself in case something were to happen. Besides, someone needs to watch the fire."

"Okay… so you're just being cautious," Tristan responded, continuing to walk with Charlemagne.

Charlemagne did not respond and took Tristan to where Miklos was with his men. They had established their own smaller camp away from them in a smaller clearing. Miklos was not dressed in his entire uniform. He had removed his smock and jacket underneath and was only in a white tank top shirt and his trousers. He also wasn't wearing his hat, which exposed his neatly trimmed light brown hair that appeared almost blonde in the sunlight.

"Miklos, if you're ready, I would like you to take Tristan fishing as we discussed yesterday," Charlemagne said.

"Certainly," Miklos responded, "a moment please."

Miklos went to his tent and fetched his jacket. He dressed himself properly and grabbed his rifle. Once he was ready, they returned to the main camp to cross through to re-enter the forest on the other side. Charlemagne split off from them and allowed Miklos to be alone with Tristan.

The forest around them was thicker and the trees were closer together. They consisted of both fir trees and another type of tree with thicker and larger branches, but a shorter trunk. It was a spruce tree. They walked a short distance and reached a wide river past a clearing of dirt behind them. The river was not deep and flowed at a mild pace. Tristan could see fish in the clearness of the water, swimming downstream.

"Have you fished before?" Miklos asked, looking to Tristan as he lowered the bag with the poles inside onto the beach of the river.

"Once with my dad about five years ago," Tristan replied, "but never again. I think I still remember the basics."

Tristan sat down and unzipped the bag. He took out the two rods as well as some bait toys and hooks.

"Charles really thought of everything when he bought this," Tristan remarked, looking at all the components, "but I don't know what he expects from us with this kind of bait."

"We can catch a smaller fish and use it to catch a bigger fish," Miklos suggested, lowering his rifle beside him before sitting down next to Tristan.

Tristan chose a smaller hook to begin with and tied it to the end of his fishing pole. He then opened the container of bait and looked at the mess of wet dirt with various live worms inside. He chose one of the worms and proceeded to wrap it around the hook.

"What kind of fish are we expecting to see in here?" Tristan wondered as he held a finger over the reel at a release button, "maybe there's some clue in that book Charles is having Diana read."

Tristan motioned his fishing rod to the left and then flicked the pole straight forward, sending the line into the water a couple of meters ahead of him. Miklos removed his jacket as they sat under the heat of the sun. He then readied his own pole and then sent cast his own line.

Within a couple of minutes, Tristan's line began to move, which forced him to grab his pole and reel. He stopped reeling, especially as the resistance stopped entirely.

"Damn, it got away," Tristan remarked, withdrawing his line to check on his bait, "and the little guy bit my worm in half."

"You tried to reel in too quickly," Miklos corrected. "Give them a moment to get the hook into their mouths."

Tristan looked to him and then adjusted the worm. He then threw his line in again to wait for another chance. The line bobbed again and Tristan gave the fish a couple of seconds before he started to reel to cut the slack. The fish continued to pull back as Tristan pulled back. He brought the fish to surface and reeled it in.

The fish he had rolled in had a small head and rounded body. Its scales were grey, but its fins and head was blue. It had two ventral fins and one dorsal fin and was approximately six inches in length.

"Not bad for the first ten minutes," Tristan remarked, showing Miklos who hardly held a smile. "This'll get us a bigger boy."

Tristan removed the small hook from the fish's mouth and then took out the larger hook from the pack. He changed his fishing pole for the larger hook. Miklos took a knife from his trousers and cut the fish Tristan had caught in half.

"What'd you do that for?" Tristan questioned.

"Dead or alive, that doesn't matter and the fish was too large to use as bait," Miklos replied, cutting off the posterior fin and tossing it back into the water. "Here."

Tristan took the anterior half of the fish and ran his hook through it. He then handed the rod to Miklos.

"Give me a minute, I'm going to take off my shoes and socks," Tristan said, doing that.

Tristan then took the pole back into his hands and walked into the river. He threw his line as far as he could towards the river and then stood in the water going up to almost his knees and shorts. Nothing came in the next couple of minutes.

Miklos was able to catch his own small fish and cut his in half just as he did with Tristan's. He then threw his own line. Tristan continued to stand, waiting for his rod to either bend or drag. Another couple of minutes passed before Tristan felt his rod pull forward.

"Hey, I've got something!" Tristan cheered, reeling the slack between the fish. "It's something big too!"

Tristan pulled his rod up and took steps back onto the beach. He continued to diminish the slack between the rod and the line while pulling the rod back at the same time. Miklos watched and stood up as he noticed Tristan struggling. Tristan kept focused eyes forward at the fish struggling in the water ahead of him. The fish was larger than the previous fish and more than a foot in length. Tristan reeled the fish in and once it was closer to the beach, he grabbed the top of his fishing line and held the fish by it.

The fish flopped around in the air and splashed both Miklos and Tristan. Tristan laughed as he held it. The fish was approximately sixteen-inches in length. The fish continued to flop its muscular tail around. It had a healthy mass and small lateral fins. The fish was grey and had whiskers.

"I didn't know they had catfish in the UK," Tristan said, holding the fish. "I thought catfish was exclusive to North America. Damn, it's too bad Diana isn't here for this – I would have loved her to take a picture of this. Hey, Miko, come grab my phone!"

Miklos caught Tristan's phone as he threw it to him and took a picture. He then put Tristan's phone into his pocket and motioned Tristan to bring the fish over to him.

"Let's put the poor thing out of its misery," Miklos suggested. "There's no sense in letting it suffer, is there?"

Miklos took the fish by the top of the line and then brought it over to the bank, setting it onto the ground and restraining it with his hands. He then punched the fish in the head, stunning it, and grabbed his knife.

"Do you want to do the honors? It's your fish after all," Miklos said, offering the knife to Tristan.

Tristan took the knife and then looked at the fish. He looked at the fish in the eyes.

"Tristan?" Miklos questioned. "Are you going to kill it or do you want me to?"

"Kill it," Tristan simply said to him.

Miklos rotated the knife in his hand, bringing the handle into his grip and then cut the fish by the gills, releasing blood and then pushed the knife into the back of the fish's head. The fish became still, which told them that it was done.

"Congratulations," Miklos said, picking up the fish and handing it to him as if it were a newborn. "It's all yours to take back to Charles."

"Thanks," Tristan replied with an awkward smile.

Act 1, Scene 5

Tristan and Miklos returned to the camp later in the morning with their catch. They were able to catch another three catfishes with the smaller fishes they had caught, which was plenty for them. Diana looked over to them returning and leaving the fishes in the bucket of water near the fire.

Charlemagne was nowhere to be seen at the moment and Lukas was at the perimeter of camp, leaning against a tree as he supervised Diana and polished his rifle. Miklos walked back up to the tents and looked to Lukas.

"Where's Mr. Cabernet?" Miklos questioned.

"He went out with Lacplesis," Lukas responded. "Igor is setting motion scanners around the outskirts of the camp."

Miklos nodded to him while Tristan went over to Diana, sitting down next to her on the beach. He gave her a quick kiss on the cheek and then looked out to the lake as she read the book Charlemagne assigned to her.

"How was it?" Diana asked, closing the book and looking at him. "Did you have fun with Miko?"

"Yeah," Tristan replied, "but only as much fun as one can have with him. He can be too serious sometimes."

"Well, that sounds like him," Diana sighed. "I wish I could have gone with you – I would have loved to have taken some pictures."

"Next time – there'll be a next time for sure," Tristan responded, taking out his phone, "but I was sure to grab a snap of my first catch."

Tristan showed Diana the picture.

"Impressive – is that a catfish?" Diana questioned.

"Yeah, I was as surprised as you – I thought they were unique to North America, like the Deep South or something, but I suppose they're pretty common like squirrels."

Tristan put his phone away.

"How's the book?" Tristan asked. "Learning much?"

"I don't know why Charles is making me read this stupid book," Diana remarked. "I feel like this is all stuff he should know."

"Charles told me he wants both of us to know the basics in case something were to happen to either of us," Tristan explained. "He's just being as cautious as usual."

"He told me he was going to make you read this thing too," Diana replied.

"I don't need to read that," Tristan responded. "Besides, I'm more of a person who learns by first-hand experience and example, not by words on paper."

"You just don't like to read," Diana scolded, smiling at him and tilting her head at him. "I couldn't get passed the first twenty-pages to be honest. I went back to reading the book I brought as I hoped to while we were here."

Tristan widened his smile, looking at Diana's book, which was *The Jungle Book* by Rudyard Kipling. The couple then turned their heads back over to Lukas and Miklos as they noticed someone rushing towards them. It was Igor. He was saying something to them and looked serious and distressed. The couple instantly stood up and went upwards to get a better listen.

"I don't know," Igor said, "but I would have to hazard that we don't have long."

"What's going on?" Diana questioned, looking to them.

"Stay here," Miklos cautioned them, taking his radio from his belt and bringing it to his mouth. "Charlie-Seven, this is

Charlie-One. Return with *Imperator* at once. I repeat, return with Charlie Actual immediately."

"Roger," Lacplesis responded from the other end.

Miklos and Lukas then looked into the forest as if they had seen something. Their weapons were readied in their arms. Igor unlatched his rifle from around his shoulder and cocked the bolt.

"Spread out," Miklos ordered, taking cover by a tree.

The others spread out to separate trees and fanned out to cover a large portion of the campsite perimeter. Elegast joined them and took cover.

Tristan and Diana laid low behind the embankment and kept their eyes scanning the ground ahead.

• • •

Charlemagne, with a rabbit trap in one hand, looked to Lacplesis as he listened to Miklos' transmission. The two were stood in the midst of the forest not too far from the camp. The ground at the feet was mixed between grass and patches of dirt. There was a thickness of shrubs around them and a heavier concentration of deciduous trees with healthy green leaves at their branches and broad brown bark trunks.

"What was that about?" Charlemagne questioned.

"I'm not sure," Lacplesis responded, taking out his rifle from behind his shoulder and readying it, "but stay behind me and I'll get you back to the camp."

Charlemagne prepared the trap in his hand and laid it down on the ground, getting down on one knee before standing up. Lacplesis ran to the nearest tree to take cover. Charlemagne then followed and hid behind him.

Once Lacplesis was sure that ahead of them was clear, he dashed forward into the next available tree before jumping to the next with Charlemagne behind him. Within ten minutes, the two had returned to the camp ahead of them. Lacplesis scanned the area ahead and then made a final dash towards the embankment where the kids were. Charlemagne rejoined the kids not too soon after.

"Is everything alright?" Charlemagne questioned as Lacplesis climbed over the embankment and went to a tree to join his comrades. "What's going on?"

"Igor apparently saw something – I'm not sure what, and they told us to lay low," Tristan replied. "I haven't seen anything yet."

Charlemagne looked to Tristan and then looked over the embankment. He heard the rustle of shrubs ahead.

"Hello?" a man yelled out in a Northumbrian accent.

Charlemagne looked to the kids and then back towards Miklos ahead. He was looking towards Lukas. He was presenting his right hand with an open fist, motioning them to stand down.

"Hello?!" the man shouted out again

Miklos relaxed his stance and brought his rifle back around his shoulder. He then exited from his cover and stepped forward.

"Good morning," Miklos yelled out. "How can I help you?"

Charlemagne stood up and went around to join Miklos. The man ahead of them was a middle-aged man, younger than Charlemagne with thin brown hair and fair skin. He was dressed in a blue coat and wore shorts with hiking boots. The front of his jacket had the logo of England's National Parks services.

"Hello," the man said again. "I'm a park warden and took notice of your campsite…"

Charlemagne caught up and looked to the man.

"What seems to the matter?" Charlemagne questioned in an aggressive manner. "We have all our paperwork for the fire, fishing rods, and even the rifles – I was sure to respect the rules and regulations of the park, so what have I missed?"

"I'm afraid it nothing like that," the ranger replied. "The matter is of a serious note, and unfortunately, due to the upspring of a forest fire in the park, I've been asked to locate and evacuate all of our tourists effective immediately. I will also have to ask that you put out your own campfire immediately to reduce the risk of any further fires spreading – afterwards, I'll see to it that you're escorted from the premises."

"This is unbelievable," Charlemagne complained. "I've travelled a great many miles to be here with my family – only for our vacation to end so soon? How could a fire have started? Who was so reckless to allow a fire to begin?"

The park warden motioned his hands for Charlemagne to calm down.

"I don't wish to point any fingers right now because the situation is being investigated and there has been no conclusive cause found. I'll be more than happy to give you more details if you'll all kindly follow me back to our station. My pickup is not too far from here."

Charlemagne sighed and didn't say any more. He simply nodded and turned to Miklos.

"I suppose we'll have to do as he says," Charlemagne said. "Let's gather our things and go with him – I want to know what, or who caused this fire."

Act 2, Scene 1

Once Charlemagne, the kids, and the mercenaries had packed up their belongings, they trekked out into the forest with the park ranger and hiked less than a mile to reach a dirt road in the middle of the forest where the ranger's vehicle was parked.

"Honestly," Charlemagne cursed, seeing the truck as they came out of the forest. "All this time, I thought we were more hidden than we were, but there was a bloody road not too far off from the camp!"

The kids were silent as they walked forward and loaded their things into the back of the truck. The front cabin only had space for four passengers, which left Lukas, Lacplesis, Igor, and Elegast in the back of the truck for the drive out of the forest, which was less than twenty minutes.

The park warden brought the group to a lodge outside of the forest, or at the entrance. A sign at the side of the road near the lodge read, 'Berwick-Northumbria National Park' in large gold font and 'Northumberland Entrance' below. The lodge was a two-story stone home with a dark grey-tiled gable roof. The station looked to have been constructed in the last twenty or so years. The home had black-framed casement windows and a spruce door. Likewise, the floorboards, railings and pillars of the porch as well as the steps to the porch were made of the same spruce wood. The front garden was neatly trimmed and included a flagpole with the Union Jack flying in the wind. To the left of the house was a large field alongside a helicopter landing pad closer to the house. The field was large and went to a large lake with some more cabins around the side. The pickup truck drove around a causeway and then off a detour to the right that led to a garage at the side of the house. Once the pickup truck was parked, the ranger led the group out of the car and into the house.

The group was led out through a tight corridor and to the front lobby via a glass door unlocked with an ID pass. In the lobby, there was an information desk to the left of the main doors and various banners in front. Next to the desk was an archway that led into a type of lounge with a table in the middle with four chairs, two at either side. Behind the table on the left were sofas facing a fireplace stove. At the opposite side of the room, behind the table in the center was a countertop desk with three computer stations, and on the last face of the room were bookshelves with a French window in the center that went into another room. In the room on the right, it was another sort of lounge, but with a kitchen and some countertops with some chairs. There were also another two tables with two chairs on either side as well as some more sofas facing a flat screen TV.

"You can make your accommodations for your people to pick you up in our learning center," the ranger said, holding the glass door that went into the rear of the station as he looked to Charlemagne.

"Now hold on," Charlemagne said, stopping the man. "You told me that you'd explain the cause of the fire – I have business in these forests and need to know for the sake of my people."

The ranger looked to Charlemagne and then nodded.

"Come on through then," the ranger said, widening the door for Charlemagne.

Charlemagne turned to Miklos.

"Wait here with the kids – get into contact with Mr. Heavner, if you can, to have our transport brought to us," Charlemagne ordered. "I'll be right back."

Miklos nodded and led the kids into the learning center. From the lobby, the ranger led Charlemagne into a large room at the center-rear of the house with a view of a small lake through some large windows, past a chain link fence outside. There were various desks in this living room, at the side of the room with a large table in the middle that included a large map of both Northumberland and Berwick with the forest in the middle. The map was topographic and included the terrain, different altitudes as well as rivers, lakes, and an area was wooded with coniferous, deciduous, mixed or any trees at all. It also included location names as well as a grid with coordinates. The map was laid out like a map of a war room with pieces of red folded paper on the map indicating the extent of the fire at the moment. The room was occupied by another park warden, a female with blonde hair who was at a desk and on a phone.

"Good, you've returned," the blonde said in a Norwich accent, looking to the man. "Defra called again and want you to call back."

"Good Lord," the male ranger responded. "I'll call them back at once."

The male ranger led Charlemagne to the table and then pointed to the location of the fire on the map. Charlemagne looked at their present location. The park stretched from an area at the top known as Hethpool and came down to an area known as Barrow Burn in England. On the opposite side of the border these areas shadowed Butterburn, a rural countryside to the north, and Leithope Forest in the south. The Scottish side consisted of farmland. To the right of Barrow Burn was a piece of the park that broke off on its own known as Otterburn after the town at the entrance of the park where they were. The entrance of the park was right at the A68 which ran through to get to the Scotland. The Scotland entrance into the park through this motorway was known as the Whitelee Entrance as it was next to the Whitelee Moor National Nature Reserve and a small reservoir on the south coast of the A68 known as Catcleugh Reservoir. In the south, in the English portion of the park up to another motorway was Tarset Forest and then Wauchope Forest in the Scottish portion. Below Wauchope Forest, in England, was Kielder Forest, the largest forest in the entire park. Across the freeway, on the north coast was Kielder Lake, which gave off to River North Tyne, which ran along the road. The freeway went from England into Scotland from a town known as Bellingham, south of Otterburn. This town included a secondary entrance into the park from England. By the lake there was a small town known as Falstone. To the right of Kielder Forest was Wark Forest and below that forest was Henshaw Forest. Below Kielder Forest was Kershope Forest. Charlemagne looked at the area where he had taken the kids. It was in the south, in Henshaw Forest. His eyes then went to where the forest fire began further north in Hethpool, slightly over in the Scottish section.

"At approximately 1930 hours last night, I received word from our fire lookout in Hethpool that he had spotted smoke rising from the west – the flames quickly spread and the incident escalated quickly to ensure that the forest didn't spread north into the urban centers. Since then, the fire has spread to the entire area… and it will most likely continue to spread as our response to this unexpected fire has been slow. By tomorrow, we're expecting it to spread towards Barrow Burn and even Leithope, and if we're not able to stop it by the A68, into Tarset and Wauchope to even Kielder and Henshaw. We're petitioning for any help we can get, so if a philanthropic billionaire such as yourself would like to make a donation to a worthwhile cause, now would be the time."

Charlemagne looked at the ranger and then back to the map.

"I can offer my current team of four mercenaries and myself – we'll do whatever it is you need from us," Charlemagne proposed. "They're professionally trained men and have been through wars and crises."

"A generous offer, Mr. Cabernet, but that was not what I meant," the ranger responded.

Charlemagne nodded and brought a hand to his neck to rub. He then looked back at the park warden.

"I own a logging industry near where the fire started," Charlemagne remarked. "I have to phone my company head and ask him if everybody is alright over here – would you mind if I used a phone?"

"Not a phone, but we have computers – you can make a webcall," the ranger suggested. "I'm afraid I must use the landline to phone Defra (The Department of Environment, Food, and Rural Affairs) who have been insisting on hourly updates. Please excuse me – we have computers that are used for educational purposes in the learning center. Feel free to use them to make your call."

"Thank you," Charlemagne responded, nodding to the ranger.

Charlemagne walked out of the map room and went down the hall and back into the public area of the house. He walked into the learning center and stood behind the kids and looked to the mercenaries.

"What time is it in Allabrese?" Charlemagne questioned, looking at his watch. "It's just about one o'clock here, which means it'll be nearing six in the morning there. Has Miklos been able to communicate with Heavner? I don't have a signal around here."

Charlemagne left the learning center and went outside to where Miklos was on a satellite phone. He was speaking to the leader of the Protection Squad, Henry Heavner, in Harlech.

"Miklos, have Heavner contact Richard Huxley and wake him," Charlemagne said. "Have Huxley video call me as soon as he gets to the office."

Miklos nodded and then continued to speak over the satellite phone. Charlemagne returned to the learning center and sat down. He turned on a computer, which invited Diana and Tristan to come over.

"What's going on?" Tristan questioned. "What are we going to do?"

"I have to get into contact with Richard and have him contact Cabernet Lumber to see if our operations in Scotland have been affected by the forest fire. We own a tiny portion of a larger operation that's part of the country's sustainable logging industry. I'm concerned about the workers and operations there."

Charlemagne logged on to the computer and then sat back in wait.

• • •

Within an hour, Charlemagne received a video call from Richard Huxley. Charlemagne answered the call and looked forward towards Richard in his office in Allabrese with a window looking out towards town square behind him.

"Charles, what seems to be problem?" Huxley questioned.

"There's been an outbreak of a forest fire here at the Berwick-Northumbria National Park. The fire originated near Hethpool Forest over the Scottish side of the park, but within less than a mile from an outpost belonging to Cabernet Lumber. I need you to get into contact with their CEO to find out what is going on, in the meantime –"

"Hold on, Charles," Richard responded, looking over his laptop and across his office. "What's going on?" he asked someone off-camera.

Charlemagne could hear the voice of someone nearby.

"Who are you talking to?" Charlemagne questioned.

"Joseph," Richard replied. "He's telling me that there's some sort of publicity crisis…"

"Our public relations haven't recovered since what I said in France, so what could possibly have arisen?" Charlemagne questioned.

Richard pushed his chair back from his computer to allow Joseph Gilbert, the Chief Communications Officer (CCO) of Cabernet Industries, to step into the view. Gilbert was a shorter than average man with slicked back dark coarse hair and fair skin. He had a sharp nose and brown eyes. He wore a grey suit and sat on Huxley's desk, crossing his arms.

"Charles," he spoke in a local accent, "Cabernet Industries is currently trending on social media in relation to the forest fire that's broken out in that park. Users are targeting us after an opinion piece criticized our lumber operations and your speech in Germany in relation to conservationism. They're all blaming us for the forest fire, stating that Cabernet Lumber was responsible for the fire."

"How horrible," Charlemagne replied. "There is no limit to these people."

"Other news sources have picked up on the trend and added, excuse the pun, fuel to the flames," Gilbert remarked. "My team is doing all that we can, but it is difficult."

"The ranger lead here has said that they're in desperate need of help to combat the fire – I offered him assistance in the form of the Protection Squad team with me, but he refused. Richard, as soon as you can, get into contact with Allodia to allocate a generous donation to National Park Services and have them communicate with them to see if there is anything else we can do to help."

"Certainly, Charles," Richard replied, "but what are you going to do? You aren't going to offer him your own aid again, are you?"

"I will insist…"

"And if he refuses again, you aren't going to go behind their back, are you?" Richard asked in concern.

"I… I do have business here that needs attending to and don't intend to leave the immediate area…" Charlemagne responded.

"Charles…" Richard scolded.

"No, this might be good," Gilbert replied. "What C.I. needs is a good story to report on, and if Charlemagne places himself on the frontline of this forest fire, helping first responders with the Protection Squad, it could make the most of this unfortunate situation."

"The last thing I want is to profit off of a tragedy," Charlemagne said. "We aren't a major news network. What if our attempts fan the flames of these peoples' conspiracies about us?"

"Let these conspiracists think what they wish – it is not them that we wish to influence, but normal people," Gilbert responded.

Richard brought his hands to his face and then removed them.

"What are you thinking, Richard?" Charlemagne questioned.

"Do whatever you wish, Charles," Richard responded. "I've given you my opinion, but the ultimate decision is up to you. I already know what you're going to do."

"I'll have a team fly to your location to document your efforts," Gilbert stated. "In the meantime, have one of your Protection Squad members, or…"

"Diana, she can document," Charlemagne remarked. "She did such a terrific job with my venture in France."

"There, then have her document your exploits until my team arrives," Gilbert said.

"Very well," Charlemagne said, nodding. "If you have anything to let me know of, go through Heavner to have it broadcasted to Miklos. I'll hopefully see the two of you before the end of the summer."

"Best of luck, Charlemagne," Gilbert replied, standing up.

Charlemagne cut off from the phone call and then stood up. He walked towards the exit of the learning center when the park ranger came to him.

"On second thought, Mr. Cabernet, I've spoken with the Defra and it seems as though I'll have to accept your offer to help if it is still available."

"It most certainly is," Charlemagne replied. "What can we do for you?"

Act 2, Scene 2

Later on the same day, Charlemagne travelled with Miklos, Lukas, Igor, Elegast, Lacplesis the kids, as well as Holger and a new recruit to the team, Hardrada, a young Norwegian boy with fair skin, blue eyes and blonde hair. The two Nords drove the light utility vehicles (LUV) from where they were stationed in Newcastle and picked the team up at the ranger station. They then drove into the forest and towards the Whitelee Entrance.

Charlemagne rode in the front vehicle, in the front passenger seat with the kids in the back and Miklos at the wheel. The others were in the second vehicle and behind them. Instead of being in his casual attire, he had changed into a uniform similar to Miklos' but of a lighter variety with less equipment holding him down. He had the same trousers and jacket as well as smock but did not have much more than that.

Miklos drove down a concrete road that was an offshoot from the A68. At either side there were tall fir trees with tall grass.

"From Whitelee, we have to hike for less than four miles to the fire lookout inland to Leithope Forest," Charlemagne said, looking at a map that was given to him of the forest. "We might just make it before sunset if we're lucky… and hopefully from there, the next day, we'll be able to move onwards towards the forest fire."

"What is your plan?" Miklos questioned as they drove.

"To help as they have asked," Charlemagne replied, "but also to distinguish who caused this fire and vindicate the company name."

"What are we doing here?" Tristan questioned.

"Because the national ministry in charge of the environment hired us to study and observe the forest fire that's broken out in Hethpool Forest."

"Why are *we* here then?" Tristan questioned. "I'm surprised you've allowed us to join."

"I asked you to travel to England to meet with me, and it wouldn't be fair to send you off," Charlemagne said back. "Besides, it's not like there is any real danger – we're with Miklos and his men, and we won't be delving into the forest fire, but only the scorched parts that have already been ravaged. It's there that I wish to investigate while everybody is busy tackling the flames."

"Yeah, that's entirely reasonable," Tristan replied, crossing his arms.

The car continued to drive along the road that went for almost a kilometer. Towards the end, they were stopped at a checkpoint manned by members of the British Armed Forces armed with assault rifles. There were approximately three of them at a single checkpoint going further along the road. Miklos lowered down a window and watched as one of the soldiers spoke into their radio

"Do you have any business in these parts?" a young soldier spoke in a Welsh accent. "If not, I'm going to have to ask you to leave."

The boy had fair skin, slightly on the darker side with brown eyes and brown hair. He also had thick eyebrows.

"Our paperwork is right here," Miklos said, presenting the papers the ranger had given to them. "We're here to help with the forest fire."

The soldier took the papers and looked through them. He then looked to his coworkers and had one come around. The boy was slightly older and had fairer skin and lighter brown hair cut short.

"Sorry, we're just going to have to take a moment to verify these," the older soldier said in a Geordie accent. "Apologies."

"No, no worry," Miklos responded in a chill tone. "It's not like there's a forest fire ravaging these precious lands. We have all the time to wait…"

The soldier looked to Miklos and to the other soldier with him. He gave the papers back to Miklos and then stood back.

"I'm sorry for the delay – go right ahead."

Miklos nodded and then closed his window. He then continued to drive through the checkpoint and continued a short distance towards the end of the road. On approach to the end, the armored cars passed a yellow school bus loaded with various young boys between the ages of fourteen to eighteen. They appeared to be dressed as some sort of scouts. Charlemagne noticed another bus of these adolescents parked at the entrance of the park, which consisted of a large parking lot in front of a gate towards a park trail. The gate was a wooden archway raised in the middle of a wooden fence along the outskirts of the forest around the perimeter of the parking lot. The parking lot was made of a smooth concrete, but the edges were a fine gravel. The path on the other side of the gate was also of the same gravel and behind the gate was a small artificial park with deciduous trees and open grass. There was also a gazebo in the middle. Behind the gazebo was the start of the trail into the wider forest park around.

Miklos parked the LUV outside of the park and then the group exited to collect their backpacks and what supplies they would need for the journey into the forest. There were additional British Army soldiers scattered around the park on guard duty. Charlemagne looked at them with unease. Miklos joined and looked to him as Diana took some pictures of the team at the entrance of the trail.

"We better move along to avoid walking in the dark," Miklos said. "Come on."

"Right," Charlemagne replied.

The team moved into the forest and came to a trail that went along for almost a kilometer before they then diverged and went into the wilderness beyond to move into Leithope Forest where there was a heavier presence and density of fir and spruce trees. There was also a rougher terrain with more slopes than they experienced in the south. The skies above were a warm orange, still clear as they have been in the first week of July.

Within an hour, Charlemagne looked out from atop of a hill and could see the fire lookout tower in the distance. The tower was approximately six-stories tall and stood on four legs. The top cabin was squared with a balcony around the entire perimeter. Between the legs were stairs that went up to the top of the tower. There were also struts between the legs in an X-pattern. Miklos picked up his binoculars hanging from his neck and looked towards the tower. He then passed his binoculars to Charlemagne.

Charlemagne looked through the binoculars and towards the interior of the cabin. The cabin was lined with windows on every side, including at the door, which gave them a clear view inside. There was no sight of anyone inside nor any lights turned on. Charlemagne handed Miklos' binoculars back and the two continued with the others downhill and across until they reached the base of the hill by the tower.

Tristan looked at his watch as they continued along and up the hill. His watch read that it was almost a quarter to ten o'clock. The incline led to the base of the tower at the top of the hill. There, they took a quick break to recharge while Miklos and Charlemagne travelled up the tower and entered inside.

The cabin was still unlit and there was nobody present. Charlemagne came around to the front door and opened it. He then entered with Miklos behind him. The two looked around and took notice of the furniture and chaos in the room. The bed was unmade, the dresser at the foot of the bed had every shelf pulled out and there were dirty dishes atop of the dining table in the center and at the desk in the opposite corner from the bed. The two stepped into the room and began to rummage through the mess.

"I don't see anything," Charlemagne noted to Miklos. "It's possible that they've left already of their own accord."

Miklos nodded and then looked to Charlemagne.

"What then? Do we continue or return to the station?" Miklos questioned.

"We were never really here to help," Charlemagne replied. "I think it'll be better if we continue on our own path. We can tell Defra that we went looking for the broad and got lost. I want to get closer to the fire though – we'll get into contact with the warden there then."

"Understood," Miklos responded, walking with Charlemagne back down to rejoin the others.

At the base of the tower, Lukas and the other mercenaries were inspecting a raft stored underneath the tower under some tarps. Lukas and them immediately looked over to Charlemagne and Miklos as they reached the bottom of the tower.

"Did you find her?" Lukas asked.

"Yes, but we left her up there," Charlemagne replied with sarcasm. "We're carrying on."

"What's the next course of action?" Lukas questioned.

"We'll set off from the tower and establish camp not far from here," Charlemagne explained. "Tomorrow, we'll push north to the forest fire."

Act 2, Scene 3

The team hiked for less than five minutes away from the tower and established camp near a river. Miklos and Charlemagne looked at the river as the kids went to their tents and other mercenaries to theirs.

"We can use those rafts at the lookout tower and half our travel time," Miklos suggested.

Charlemagne nodded.

"We'll set off in the morning," Charlemagne said. "I'll see you then – I need to have a word with Tristan before I retire for the night."

"Yes, sir," Miklos responded, leaving.

Charlemagne continued to look at the river. He then returned to the camp and went to Tristan's tent.

"Tristan," Charlemagne said in a quiet voice.

Tristan heard Charlemagne. He was in his sleeping bag and attempting to fall asleep. He turned on his flashlight and crawled out, unzipping his tent door and looking to Charlemagne. Tristan was dressed in a grey t-shirt and in black gym shorts. His gold necklace was buried within his shirt, but the back of the necklace was exposed by the back of his neck.

"What's up?" Tristan questioned.

"Walk with me," Charlemagne requested. "I have something I need to talk to you about in private."

Tristan looked to Charlemagne who held a serious face. All Tristan did was nod and put on his shoes. He then grabbed a jacket and walked with Charlemagne away from the camp. He brought his flashlight with him. Once they were a fair distance from the others, Tristan looked to Charlemagne.

"What did you want to talk to me about?" Tristan asked.

"What you said to me this morning has been on my mind," Charlemagne replied. "Although I was a little surprised, I am grateful nonetheless that you showed confidence in me to confess your attraction towards Diana to me."

"Yeah," Tristan responded to him. "It's no problem. I'm glad you told me how you felt about it."

"It would only be fair if I was wholeheartedly honest with you as well," Charlemagne proposed, "especially with my activities in the last two months."

"What? Were you never really travelling Europe?" Tristan asked, stopping with him in the middle of the forest. "Were you not giving speeches?"

"The dishonesty was never in what I was saying to you, but in what I was keeping hidden," Charlemagne explained. "Last spring, when we were travelling with Manon, she and I had a moment of life or death in Fort Saint-Jean where she confessed to me something that she herself had been keeping hidden to me for the last nineteen years. She was pregnant when I left her," he confessed to him. "I have a son – somewhere out there, there is a boy that I fathered with her, and the last two months since Judith's death have not merely been in mourning, or in spreading political discourse on the importance of European blood and culture, but in searching for this boy. And my liaison with Manon has not been a friendly attempt to stay connected, but my obsessive compulsion to learn as much as I can from her about who adopted our child and where he could possibly be."

"Why do you want to find him?" Tristan asked.

"Wouldn't you want the same?" Charlemagne questioned. "If your own father, you had never known, was out there somewhere, would you not want him to find you?"

Tristan stuttered to answer.

"He's my son," Charlemagne went on, "ever since I adopted both you and Diana, I have known nothing more than the importance and joy in raising you two. It's a part of the reason why my eyes have opened to see the world in a different light to when I was in my midlife crisis even before. I have, for once in my life, found peace in what the meaning of life is – it is life itself."

Charlemagne went quiet for a moment.

"That's why we're here, isn't it?" Tristan said. "We're here because he's here – your son. You don't care about the forest fire, or what Cabernet Industries is going through. You only care about your son."

"Please do not share this with anyone else," Charlemagne requested, "and by that, I mean with Diana. It is important that you do not mention this to her…"

Charlemagne took a deep breath and then brought a hand to Tristan's shoulder.

"You have grown a great amount in the last two years under my care – you have grown to be both taller and leaner than me – so physically, you have matured, but perhaps you don't understand because your mind is not there yet…"

"My mind?" Tristan questioned as they started to walk back to the camp.

"I hope that my influence is enough that one day, you may understand."

The two looked at each other again. Charlemagne stood in front of Tristan. The two looked at each other and the discrepancy in their height was noticeable by the way Tristan tilted his head down and Charlemagne tilted his head up. The two looked at each other for a few seconds before they returned to the camp.

"Goodnight," Charlemagne said to Tristan before they parted.

"Goodnight," Tristan replied, returning to his tent.

Charlemagne watched Tristan go to his tent and then gave a sigh. Tristan zipped his tent door closed and then went back to his. He got back into his sleeping bag and turned off his flashlight. He lied down on his side and kept his eyes open for a few minutes before closing them and drifting to sleep.

Act 2, Scene 4

The next morning, Charlemagne, Miklos, and some mercenaries returned to the fire lookout tower to see if the lookout had returned overnight. They came to the top of the tower to the same sight – an empty room and returned to the ground floor to retrieve the large raft. The raft was yellow and had a blue streak across the middle, around the entire perimeter. Near the raft were crates with orange life vests and plastic yellow paddles. The Protection Squad loaded the raft with the appropriate material, enough life vests and paddles for the entire group, and then carried the raft back to the camp and laid it down at the beach by the river.

In the morning daylight, the river was clear and gently streaming along. On the opposite side of the beach was a hill with fir and pine trees as well as various bushes along. The beach was composed of dirt that was consistent with the bottom of the river. There was also some grass along the sides of the beach that went into the water. The grass was tall.

By the time the team had returned to the camp, Tristan and Diana had readied themselves to carry on with the adventure. They joined them at the beach where they were checking their maps to make sure they went the right direction. Charlemagne traced his finger along the river on the map, passing the right forks to reach where they wanted to go. He then looked to the kids and pointed to the contents inside the raft.

"Children, take a life vest before you board," Charlemagne ordered.

Tristan looked at the life vests and picked one up. He then looked back to Charlemagne.

"Diana and I both know how to swim, and Diana is a lifeguard," Tristan explained. "I don't think we need life vests – the water is as calm as the lake we camped at…"

"Do not argue with me, Tristan," Charlemagne warned. "I'm not one to take chances right now. It's either wear the vest or be escorted back to Newcastle by Lukas and Brandan."

Tristan looked to Charlemagne as he looked back at the map to focus with Miklos. Tristan then looked over to Lukas and Elegast (Brandan) as they stood idle.

"Just wear the damn vest," Diana reasoned to Tristan.

Tristan looked to her and then back to Charlemagne with a resentful look. He removed his backpack and dressed himself in the life vest. He then sat down in the raft and waited for the others to finish planning their route. Diana sat down in the raft next to Tristan, on his right. They sat at the back of the raft and left the rest of the space for the mercenaries. Once Miklos and Charlemagne were done, they went over and sat down in the front of the boat. Charlemagne removed his backpack and brought it behind him. He then dressed himself in a life vest.

None of the Protection Squad members wore life vests, and in fairness, their uniforms restricted them from doing so between the bulletproof vest and the pockets of gear they had around their torsos. Lukas and Igor sat behind Charlemagne. Hardrada and Holger sat behind them. Elegast was left to push them into the water before rushing in to sit between the Nords and the kids. Tristan held onto his backpack in front of him. Diana held onto her own backpack but had her camera out on a sling around her neck.

Once the raft was in the water, the mercenaries proceeded to row them forward and towards the center of the river. From there, they then turned to face ahead. The river pushed them at a gradual pace down the river before the mercs took over and fastened the speed at which they would travel at.

The sun shined hard and there was a calmness in the ambience. All that could be heard was gentle flow of the river and chirps of birds in the trees. The men of the Protection Squad rowed for almost an hour when the waters became a little more active than when they got in. The banks of the river consisting of grass and gravel or dirt beaches were soon becoming replaced with rocky cliffs and jagged rocks protruding through the water. Within only a couple more minutes, they had drifted into rough whitewater rapids.

Diana and Tristan held on as they slid through the waters. Diana opened her backpack and brought out a raincoat she was mocked for bringing with her. Tristan did the same, took out a navy blue raincoat from his backpack given to him by the park warden and brought it over him to shield from some of the water. The raft went upwards and downwards with the waves and water splashed into the raft. Charlemagne held a serious face and gritted his teeth as he faced the whitewater ahead of him. He lowered his head as a large wave flew at them.

"The waters are too much for us," Charlemagne shouted to Miklos. "We need to disembark!"

"It's not so easy!" Miklos responded. "There are no beaches for us to run into! We will need to endure until then!"

The raft continued to flow down the rough waters when it started to tip to the left and hit against the sharp edges of a rocky cliffside. The raft then proceeded to float backwards until the Protection Squad managed to steer the raft back into the right direction. At that moment, they came over a large drop in the water, facing down and becoming soaked with water that passed through. The raft then went towards a large boulder on the right in the water, hitting it and resulting in the raft turning again before running over a large boulder near the rear. The shock caused Diana to tip over towards Tristan and for Tristan to tip over towards the water. Elegast wrapped his arms around Tristan and pulled him back, but in the process of doing so, lost his paddle. He continued to hold on to Tristan, extending another arm to hold onto Diana as they went through another series of turbulent drops in the water.

For a moment, the raft gained a slight momentum of air as it flew forward before dumping down into the water and continuing on. Elegast let go of the kids as the waters calmed out for a brief moment with a clearing of simple whitewater before them and a sight of further rocks in the distance. At the end, the raft came down another steep drop of at least ten inches before continuing onwards to further, but small drops with rocks at the sides. The raft began to turn onto its left side again as they continued along.

The Protection Squad lifted their paddles at the sight of another waterfall ahead of them and the raft went over, tipping onto its opposite side. They went over the fall and turned the raft back into the right direction as they continued along, coming to another set of steep rocks.

The rear of the raft bumped into another large boulder in the water, causing Diana to lose grip as she flew up by an inch and almost fell overboard. Elegast grabbed her at the same time as when they came over another steep waterfall of at least ten inches. The raft tipped over and fell in, water rushing through the boat. The boat turned to the right as they came to another drop soon afterwards. Tristan shielded his head as he faced the water before him as they plunged sideways. The water brushed him and he felt his body turn to the left as well as his grip in the raft disappear.

Diana saw with her own eyes as Tristan was sucked into the river.

"Tristan!" Diana shouted.

Tristan flipped and bumped into the bottom of the raft. He quickly submerged for a gasp of air and looked over to the raft ahead. He was then taken down again into the water. Charlemagne looked around and spotted Tristan behind them. He stood up and quickly sat down again, but attempted to maintain his body so that he could both see Tristan and not fall into the water.

"Tristan!" Charlemagne shouted. "Keep your feet up and stay on your back! We're going to help you!"

Charlemagne then looked to Miklos. Tristan attempted to bring his back into the water so that he could bring his feet up as Charlemagne had told him.

"We need to help him!" Charlemagne said to him.

"Say no more," Miklos responded, taking his paddle with both hands.

"I'll help him – I'm closer," Elegast argued to Miklos.

"Stay where you are – hold on to Diana," Charlemagne countered. "Miklos, please save him."

Miklos pushed through the others and came to the back of the raft. He then jumped into the water with a hand on the raft and another at the paddle, extending over towards Tristan as he began to float past them.

"Grab on!" Miklos shouted to him.

Tristan saw the paddle ahead and attempted to take it with both hands. Instead, he missed and plunged into the water. Miklos let go of the paddle and attempted to grab at Tristan's hand, but he too missed. Tristan had fallen deep into the water and was pushed through the current, under the raft and upwards at the other side. Charlemagne saw as Tristan emerged and stood up to attempt to grab him. He then looked ahead as he saw the fork in the river.

Miklos came back into the raft and took Charlemagne's paddle as joined him at the bow of the boat. He then plunged into the water with a hand on a handle and extended the paddle towards Tristan.

"Tristan!" Miklos yelled to him.

Tristan saw the paddle and extended both arms to grab it. Tristan's hands slipped as he tried to hold on to the blade. He lost his grip as they went down a drop and he rolled. Charlemagne quickly pulled Miklos into the raft as they too went over. The raft then went towards the right, splitting from the main river. Everybody looked around for Tristan, but he couldn't be seen.

"Where is he?" Charlemagne questioned, looking around. "Where is he?!"

Tristan could hear Charlemagne's shout from underneath the water of the river. The current pushed him forward and then upwards by the buoyancy of his life vest. However, by then, he was on the opposite side of the river, on the other path and going an entirely different direction. The rapids continued with Tristan attempting to maintain himself as best as possible on his back. He was pushed against a series of boulders and felt his head smash into the rock. At that moment, everything went dark.

Act 2, Scene 5

Tristan woke up to the sensation of water gently brushing at his ankles. His face was atop of a smooth, but wet beach and ambience around him was quiet. Tristan brought a hand to his head and closed his eyes. He felt a gentle wind come over him. He opened his eyes again and looked upwards to the leaves of the oak and birch trees around him, and then further beyond to the clear sky and sun shining down on him. Tristan then lowered his hand from his head and began to push himself up to sit up.

The river ahead of him was as calm as the portion they had camped along last night and woken to the same morning. Across the river was a smaller beach with a ridge, and above the ridge, a row of trees and shrubs going into the dense forest.

Tristan proceeded to examine himself, noting his shoes, shorts, and entire self to be wet with the exception of the raincoat. He removed the coat and then started to remove the life vest, tossing it to the side. He then removed his t-shirt and squeezed it in an attempt to get water out. Afterwards, he started to use it to dry his body as if it were a towel. He then shook his head, but stopped doing so soon into the action, closing his eyes as if in pain. He cleaned his face with his shirt and then turned around, looking into the forest behind him as if he had heard something. Tristan examined the area head of him with careful eyes and then took short, but concentrated breaths as if he smelt something. The short breaths were followed by deep breath from his mouth.

Ahead of him was some smoke rising from the ground. Near the smoke was a green triangular prism tent pitched into the earth. There was nobody present in the immediate area ahead, which caused Tristan to continue to examine the space ahead of him. He then took his shirt, stretched it out and put it back on before continuing towards the mysterious abandoned camp.

Tristan came to the fire and saw that it was lit in a hole in the ground with a neighboring hole next to it. Atop of the fire, across the ground, was a grid with a pan cooking some fillets of fish. The fish on the pan was of a pinkish meat. Tristan looked at the fish and then around the surrounding area to see if he could find the owner of the camp. He then looked over to a large backpack laying on the ground with a rectangular bag next to it. Atop of the bag was a boy scout uniform shirt with a neckerchief next to it. Tristan went over to it and began to look through the bag underneath but stopped himself from thoroughly searching through the bag as he looked back at the fish starting to burn. Next to the fire were some cooking utensils laid out over a dish towel. Tristan took the pan and brought it out of the fire and onto the ground next to it. He then poked at the meat to see if both sides were cooked. Tristan then sat down and gave another look around. His stomach grumbled.

Nobody was present. Tristan picked up a titanium fork near the utensils and poked into the fish. He then brought a piece towards his mouth before lowering it as he heard a rustle in the tree above him. Tristan looked above and saw a figure atop of a branch, jumping down towards him and landing atop of him.

"Get your hands off my fish!" the figure shouted, speaking in a deep Suffolk accent.

Tristan was brought onto his back by the mysterious figure who grabbed him by his wrists. Tristan looked at the boy and saw that he was young, noticeably older than Tristan, but not by a year or more. He had fair, light skin and dirty blonde hair. His face was square shaped with smooth angles and a pointed chin. His cheeks were flat. He also had a medium-sized refined nose. His hair was long like Tristan's and styled so that the fringe was to the side and textured like dry grass – light in weight and similar in color. The front of his hair was waved to the side with strands reaching the corner of his left eye. He had natural straight eyebrows and was clean-shaven, although his face was not smooth. The boy was dressed in a white tank top shirt tucked into brown shorts with a black belt around. At his belt was a knife in a brown pouch. He appeared to be of the same build as Tristan and almost the same height, but on the shorter side.

The two struggled with each other until Tristan was able to knock him to his side and then proceed to stand up. The boy stood up and ran at Tristan, tackling him onto the ground. The boy threw a punch at Tristan, but Tristan caught it with his hand and then pushed the boy back. Tristan then stood up as the boy went forward to tackle him again. Tristan caught the boy's hands and the two struggled with each other, looking at one another with serious faces.

The boy looked at Tristan intently and his eyes moved side to side as he scanned him. He then eased his force and pushed Tristan back with a gentle push.

"You're not a warden," the boy said to Tristan. "You're too young to be one. How come you're dressed in that coat?"

"I was with them – I was with some people who were contracted by them – they gave me the coat," Tristan explained. "I'm not with them though – that was just my adoptive father."

"Are they near? Where are they?" the boy then questioned.

"No, they're not – at least I don't think so. I was separated from them while we were coming down the river – I fell in the water and I think I hit my head too… I just woke up on the beach over there. They're here to help out with the forest fire…"

"You were separated?" the boy asked, relaxing himself.

"Yes," Tristan responded, "I'm sorry I tried to eat your fish, but it was burning and I was hungry."

The boy looked at the fish and then back to Tristan.

"It's alright," the boy said to him. "I bet you were hungry... I can share."

"Thanks..." Tristan replied, watching him as he crouched down to split the fish onto a plate. "You're a boy scout? I saw some of them when we entered the forest entrance."

"I was separated from them..." the boy explained, standing up and handing the plate over to Tristan. "I... I was doing some fishing and lost track of time – but it's alright. I'm fine."

Tristan took the plate. The boy then invited him to sit down and eat with him. Tristan dug into the fish, which turned out to be Atlantic salmon. Once Tristan was done, he lowered the plate and looked over to the boy as he continued to eat.

"Thanks for that," Tristan said to the boy. "What's your name?"

The boy looked to Tristan. He was sat at the opposite-side of the fire with his knees together and bent. He swallowed the food in his mouth.

"Finn," the boy said, "you?"

"Tristan," Tristan replied.

"Well, it's nice to meet you, Tristan," Finn said. "What brings you to a place like Berwick-Northumbria? Let alone England."

"Family," Tristan responded. "My... sister and I came to England from Canada – we're on vacation. We're from a small town in a place known as Alberta. We came here to meet with my adoptive-father, and we were doing some camping until we were evacuated by a warden due to the fires."

"Sorry," Finn replied, "about the fires – not that I set them. It's a shame your family's holiday was interrupted by the travesty. Do you know how they started?"

"No..." Tristan responded.

"Pigs," Finn stated. "Pigs in suits who've sacrificed this forest for the sake of their own greed. The area where the fire started is rich in natural resources below all those trees, and if the fire clears them out, then the area loses its value as a park and can become sold by the government to recover from the costs of these rescue parties, firefighting efforts, and the sort."

"How do you know?" Tristan questioned.

"Because my father is one of those scumbags," Finn replied. "He's a rich industrialist and owner of a billion-dollar corporation with stakes in these lands…"

Tristan looked at Finn with intent. He looked at Finn straight into his eyes and then at his hair, his face, and his build.

"How old are you? Tristan asked.

"Eighteen," Finn answered, "but I'll be nineteen in September."

"Interesting…" Tristan replied, looking down at the fire pit.

"What's interesting?" Finn questioned.

"You remind me of someone," Tristan simply said, "it's uncanny how similar you are to him."

"Alright…" Finn replied, "well, honestly, if you want to come with me, I can take you to the nearest park station so that they can get you back to your folks."

"Thanks," Tristan responded, "that would be nice. I suppose it'd be safer if we stuck together. I'm not very savvy when it comes to being outdoors and only know the basics of camping."

"It's no problem," Finn said with a light smile, looking at the fire pit. "I'm a survivalist – I'll make sure that you get back home safe."

"Thanks…" Tristan said, looking at Finn, "my alternative would have been to just stay here until my adoptive-father came looking for me."

"Nah, that's dangerous," Finn replied. "You'd be taking a gamble if you stayed here. There's no guarantee your dad's mates are going to find you. Come with me and I'll take you to the right place. Let me help you out of those wet rags you're wearing though – it's not good for you to be in wet clothing like that…"

"Do you have spare clothing?" Tristan questioned.

"Of course I do," Finn responded, standing up and going to his backpack. "We're about the same size – I'll let you wear something while we let them garbs of yours dry up in the sun. Afterwards, we'll head on out so that you can get back to your sister and dad."

Finn dug around in his large backpack near his tent and took out a pair of shorts. He also fetched a towel and a white shirt. Tristan stood up and went over to him.

"Here," Finn said, handing him the items.

"Thanks," Tristan replied, taking the items and standing awkwardly as Finn sorted his items.

Tristan took a step back from Finn and looked around. He then proceeded to remove his coat and throw it on the ground before removing his t-shirt and tossing it onto the ground too. He then started to dry his torso with the towel before removing his shorts. He kept his wet boxers on and simply changed into the shorts and t-shirt before going to where Finn had a wire line between two trees. Tristan hung his clothing in the sun, and as he was setting them, he looked to the beach and towards his life vest that he had left. He then looked back to the camp.

Finn had dismantled his tent and was already almost finished packing his things. He went back to Finn.

"I left something on the beach – I'll be right back," Tristan explained to him.

"Sure," Finn replied, stuffing some things into his backpack, "do you mind fetching some water in that bucket over there?"

"Yeah," Tristan replied, picking up the bucket.

Tristan went back to the beach and looked back to see if Finn was looking towards him. He was not. Tristan knelt down on the sand and began to write with his fingers a brief message. He then took the life vest and left it over the writing in the sand. Once he was done, he took the bucket and went to the river, scooping some water and then returning to hand it to Finn.

Finn poured the water into the fire pit he had constructed, extinguishing the fire and causing a whirl of smoke to rise up.

"No point in letting that run," Finn stated, lowering the bucket and picking up a long wooden pole with a piece of string attached at the top in one hand, and a cylindrical white bag in the other. "Come on, while your clothes are drying, let's go for a walk around. There's something I want to show you."

Act 3, Scene 1

Tristan and Finn walked out from the camp and went a short distance towards a small clearing with a turned over. Tristan looked across the clearing and over to some trees which had their trunks chafed as if someone had stabbed at them a couple times. Finn laid the bag down on the log in front of them, turned over on its side, and then looked to Tristan.

"What do you want to show me?" Tristan questioned.

"Do you know what this is?" Finn asked, poking the polished wooden pole in his hand into the ground.

"No…"

"It's a bow," Finn answered. "A longbow to be specific if it wasn't obvious. A national pastime of the English."

"Is yours broken?" Tristan questioned.

"No, it's just undone for ease of transport," Finn replied, turning the pole around and bringing the top of the pole with the string to his shoe. "All I need to do to assemble it is to brace the string."

Finn took the other end of the string, the part that was not attached with his one hand, securing the opposite end of the bow at his shoe, and with his other hand at the other end, he started to stretch the bow out, arching it into a D-shape. Finn then secured the loose bit of string around a groove at the top and then picked up the bow to show Tristan.

The longbow was as tall as either of them, but thin and seemingly light.

"So simple, and yet so beautiful," Finn romanticized. "A bit of wood and a bit of string."

"Did you make that bow yourself?" Tristan questioned, unimpressed.

"Yes – it took a lot of hours of hard work – days really," Finn expressed, admiring his bow with a pleasant smile on his face. "You see this wood? It's a type of wood known as yew – that's what the traditional bows that English longbowman used were made of."

Finn caressed the wood, running the back of his hand along the side of the polished, reddish-brown wood.

"Have you ever seen a yew tree? Do they have them in Canada?" Finn asked.

"I'm not sure," Tristan replied, crossing his arms and looking to Finn with a bored face. "What's the string made of?"

"Linen – just plain old linen," Finn answered, looking at the string and bringing his finger to touch the string.

Finn showed off the tightness of the string as he tugged at it like a guitar string. The string was firm.

"So simple, and yet this deadly weapon was the bane of the French during the Battle of Agincourt in the Hundred Years' War," Finn explained. "They were the bane of knights, period, because longbowman were powerful people who could kill a knight from such a long distance – two hundred, maybe three hundred yards away with ten arrows firing every half a minute, and there were not just one of them," he added, squatting down to open the bag on the log with arrows inside and bringing the bag to his belt, "there was a whole group of them and they were commoners – everyday people who were killing noblemen."

Finn brought his hand to the center of the bow, the handle, and then with two fingers at either side of the nock of the arrow, he drew the string back with the bow atop of the handle. He then fired the first arrow, sending it flying forward and piercing the tree at the other side of the clearing. The arrow stuck out from the tree as Finn picked up another arrow to reload.

"I've been doing nothing this morning but firing away," Finn explained to Tristan who still seemed unempathetic or even sympathetic. "Back in the day, people had their young train on these for hours on end from the age of seven, maybe even five-years old, honing their skills."

Finn continued to fire arrows.

"Isn't it a soothing thought to think that life was so simple for them? Where they had no other worries but could simply do that for the entire day?" Finn questioned. "Peasants in the older days had less worries than us – they were less miserable."

"There's nothing cheerful about poor sanitation and a low life expectancy," Tristan finally said. "No offense, but what's the difference between their constraint of time and yours? You're right here shooting a bow without a care in the world."

Finn looked to Tristan after he shot his last arrow. There were still around ten more in the bag at his waist. Finn looked down and lowered the bow so that it was pointed at the ground in front of him. He then turned back forward and relaxed from his firing position.

"Why don't you give it a shot?" Finn said to Tristan. "I want to see how you're at it – you look like a natural athlete."

"Thanks, but I don't know the first thing about archery," Tristan responded.

"Then I'll teach you," Finn insisted, handing him the bow. "Come on."

Tristan took the bow into his hand by the handle. He noticed it to be lighter than he expected. Tristan then stepped forward to where Finn had been standing and looked ahead to the trees being used as targets.

"First off, you need to take a correct stance," Finn explained. "A comfortable one – there's no perfect stance and it's really whatever you feel comfortable with. I prefer to stand with by body slightly angled, like this."

Finn stood next to Tristan with his body angled so that his left side was pointed forward and his left foot was forward.

"You need to have your feet planted firmly in the ground and be able to look forward towards your target," Finn further explained.

Tristan mimicked Finn's stance and then looked forward to the targets again.

"Then, you bring the bow up with your right, pointed straight forward so that the bow is straight and your body is straight," Finn said to Tristan, holding his hand out as if he had an imaginary bow in his hand.

Tristan pointed the bow forward. Finn broke his stance and looked to him. He then went behind him and brought his hands to his chest to straighten Tristan's back. Finn then backed off and continued to look forward, beyond Tristan to where Tristan was looking. Finn took the bag at his belt and fixed it to Tristan's belt.

"It's fiction that an archer has his arrows around his back for ease of use in a quiver – it's not easy to pull an arrow from behind your back. The correct place to keep 'em is at your side. Take an arrow."

Tristan took an arrow.

"Now, with two fingers, one at either side of the end of the arrow, bring the tip atop of the handle, above your hand, and using the same two fingers at the end, pull at the string, but don't fire."

Tristan rested the tip of the arrow, the front of the shaft along the handle and then hooked his two fingers at the string so that he could pull.

"Hold this position," Finn said, lowering his voice as he spoke to Tristan, "and let it melt in your mind. Let your muscles remember this position – now pull back…. more or else that arrow won't go anywhere. Find your anchor point, the point where you want to hold and where you want to stretch back to."

Tristan drew the string even further from where he had brought it to close to parallel to his left ear, bringing it further to his right. He felt his arm shaken as his muscles were contracted for a continuous period of time.

"Eye your target, keep focused on your target," Finn whispered to him. "Aim."

Tristan aimed at a tree, near one of Finn's earlier arrows.

"And release."

Tristan let go and felt the arrow race off and shoot forward towards the target, but land short and pitch itself in the dirt about halfway. Finn gave a half frown and smile as he took a side step from behind Tristan to look. Tristan only gave a full frown as he lowered the bow and relaxed.

"Keep at it," Finn encouraged. "I didn't expect your first to be spot on. I'm going to go fetch some more arrows…"

Tristan turned his neck as Finn left. He then took a deep breath as he looked ahead. He fired a second arrow but missed. He fired a third. It landed almost three-quarters to the target. Tristan repositioned his angle so that it was a little more tilted upwards. He fired a fourth and missed the tree but was on the same perpendicular plane. There he remained as he wasted the rest of his six remaining arrows, missing the target, but raining arrows around until Finn returned with more arrows. Tristan lowered the bow and looked to him.

Finn grabbed some arrows from the second bag he had by the handful and brought them into Tristan's bag at his waist.

"I can't hit the target," Tristan confessed.

"No worries," Finn responded, looking forward. "Keep at it – you'll get there."

Tristan took a deep breath and grabbed an arrow. He pulled it back with Finn watching his movement.

"Instead of pulling back like that," Finn recommended, "take the arrow and bring your arm up so that you're pulling with your shoulder and back. Archery is a back-muscle intensive exercise."

Tristan relaxed the arrow in the bow and tried again.

"Focus on shoulder and back muscles here," Finn said, bringing the palm of his hand to Tristan's posterior deltoid, trapezoid, and teres muscles of the back. "Focus your mind of these muscles – also focus on the target but keep conscious of your muscles – envision the contraction of those muscles as you pull back. Squeeze at them."

Finn squeezed at Tristan's muscles with his hand. Tristan fired another arrow. The arrow passed the tree on the left-side by about a meter.

"Stay focused on the target. Readjust your aim, but don't forget about those key muscles," Finn said in a calming and soothe voice, moving his hands away from Tristan's back. "You need to keep a muscle-mind connection as if you're pressing weights in a gym. You can hit that target – I know you can if you believe in yourself. You got to have confidence in yourself."

Tristan fired another arrow. The arrow pierced the bottom of the tree trunk.

"Nice," Finn said, slapping Tristan in the back, "not bad, rookie. You've got it!"

Tristan gave a shy smile and then looked to Tristan who was smiling at him.

"You just got to keep practicing and hold that confidence," Finn smiled.

The two continued to practice for almost two hours. Finn would continue to coach Tristan and fetch the arrows from the field once they were out. At the start of the sun beginning to set, they returned to the camp and Finn finished putting his things away while Tristan looked at his clothes and then back to the beach. Finn put on his boy scout shirt, but didn't button up. He then looked to Tristan. Tristan looked back at him.

Finn had a large backpack that just about fit everything inside apart from the rectangular bag with a strap that went around his shoulder. The longbow was undone and fitted through some loops on one side and the bags of arrows hung via clips on the other side.

"I can help you with some of that gear," Tristan suggested, walking over to him with his clothes. "I can take that pack of yours in the least."

"Sure," Finn replied, removing the rectangular pack and handing it to Tristan. "I'll also get you something to put your clothes in.

Finn removed his backpack and dug through it to produce some string, a large three-foot by three-foot cloth, and then laid it on the ground.

"Place your crap in here – I've also got some other rubbish for you to carry if you can," Finn said, rummaging through his backpack to take out items in plastic bags to toss in the bag. Tristan folded and laid his spare clothes atop of the bag. Finn put some of his clothing and then took two medium-sized rocks from the ground nearby and placed them at opposing corners. He then folded each corner over the rock and folded the bag so that he had a cylindrical lump. With each ends of the string, he tied around the necks of the knobs formed by the rocks, creating a makeshift backpack for Tristan to carry. Finn then picked up the pack and handed it to Tristan.

"Here you are," Finn said, handing it to him. "I hope that's alright."

"Thanks," Tristan responded.

"Come on, I want to get a fair distance covered before the sun sets – I don't want to have to waste batteries on my torches because we were too busy faffing around. We'll then set camp and have some of our leftover salmon from lunch – after that, we're going to have to do a little bit of hunting."

"Sure thing," Tristan replied, latching the bag behind his back and looking to Tristan. "Let's go then."

Act 3, Scene 2

Charlemagne and the others endured the whitewater rapids for another kilometer before the waters started to smooth out. The raft was brought to a low cliff where they got out before pulling the raft upwards onto the rock. The Protection Squad took a moment to recover while Charlemagne went to the raft and pulled out Tristan's backpack.

"I want a search party organized to look for him," Charlemagne ordered. "Finding Tristan is the highest priority as of now, and I will not rest until he is found."

Charlemagne took out his map from his jacket and laid it out on the rock. He traced from the fork in the river to the end.

"Yes, Charles," Miklos replied. "I'll phone Mr. McGarrick and have a helicopter brought in – we'll start our search from where we last saw him."

"We'll need to move fast," Charlemagne replied. "There's lots of ground to cover – split your team. We'll establish camp near here and have half garrisoned with Diana while we look for him."

"Of course," Miklos confirmed.

Diana sat in the corner with one knee up. She rested her chin on her left knee and looked out to the water depressingly. Charlemagne looked to her and took a deep sigh.

• • •

Within a couple of minutes, the team set off from the river and established a camp in the forest not too far from the water. A light helicopter flew over them and then landed in a nearby clearing, ready to assist Charlemagne in the search for Tristan. Charlemagne boarded with the pilot while Miklos, Igor,

Lacplesis, Holger, and Hardrada sat on outboard benches on the side.

Diana watched with Lukas and Brandan with her as the others left. She held the same saddened look on her face as she saw the helicopter raise up and fly off. From the camp they had established to the north, the helicopter flew towards the river and proceeded to follow it back to the fork where they had lost Tristan.

"There's two possibilities for Tristan's fate!" Charlemagne briefed the team with a cold face. "Either he's drowned or he's managed to survive. I refuse to believe that Tristan had allowed himself to drown, so the most likely is the latter scenario, which means he's waiting for us somewhere near the river. I want two teams to hike the length of the river from where we lost him!"

"Yes, Charles," Miklos responded.

Once at the fork, the helicopter lowered near a beach to allow Lacplesis and Igor off to start a search via land on the right-side. The helicopter then moved to the left-side for Holger and Hardrada to get off and search the left-side. The helicopter then rose upwards near the fork.

"Follow the river!" Charlemagne shouted to the pilot. "And keep a low level!"

"Yes, Mr. Cabernet!" the pilot replied.

The helicopter proceeded to follow the river northwards. In comparison to the opposite side where Charlemagne had gone to, the side that Tristan had gone was shorter and bended to the east. The helicopter flew the entire length of the river, but Charlemagne could not see anything that positively resembled Tristan.

Charlemagne had the helicopter fly the length of the river three times before he rested. The sun started to set for them as they returned to the fork. Charlemagne looked around.

"What about another strategy?!" Charlemagne questioned both the pilot and Miklos. "If we use infrared sensors, we could better identify any living object below!"

"It'll take time to deploy something along those lines!" Miklos replied.

Charlemagne frowned.

"What if he's drowned…" Charlemagne said, shaking his head. "Even then, his body would have floated to a beach or something."

Charlemagne sighed.

"Once more – let's fly the length once more," Charlemagne insisted.

"Charles…" Miklos responded. "We've flown three times already – he's not anywhere near."

"Well then where is he?!" Charlemagne questioned. "Tristan isn't stupid. He wouldn't have wandered away! He knows we would set off looking for him!"

The helicopter stayed where it was.

"Fly the damn course!" Charlemagne ordered the pilot.

"Yes, Mr. Cabernet," the pilot responded.

"And delve as low as you can!" Charlemagne added. "I want to be able to feel the mist of the river on my face!"

The helicopter lowered towards the surface of the river. It awkwardly inserted itself between the trees, narrowly avoiding collision. The pilot then pushed forward. Charlemagne kept his eyes to the left while Miklos looked to the right. The helicopter followed the rapids up to a point where the waters began to calm down to the east. Charlemagne kept focused, but didn't see anything.

"Hold on," Miklos said, banging his fist into the side of the helicopter. "I see something – over there!"

Miklos pointed. Charlemagne looked past the pilot but couldn't see.

"What do you see?!" Charlemagne questioned.

"Some debris – something washed up on the river," Miklos observed. "It looks like Tristan's life vest."

"Take us over there!" Charlemagne ordered the pilot.

"I can't go any closer," the pilot complained. "I'll need to pull up and find somewhere to land!"

"Go on then!" Charlemagne responded. "Hurry!"

The pilot brought the helicopter upwards. He then pushed forward to a small clearing nearby. The light helicopter flew down and landed in the small field. Miklos set off towards the beach and Charlemagne joined him.

The two came to the edge of the forest and proceeded along. Miklos kept track of their location with the GPS mounted to his wrist. Meanwhile, Charlemagne looked around their surroundings. They were in a deciduous forest with dirt composing most of the ground and a lack of shrubby nearby. Charlemagne noticed a hole in the ground with burnt wood.

"Hold on," Charlemagne said to Miklos, walking over to the hole. "Look."

Miklos saw the hole and joined Charlemagne.

"Someone had a fire here," Charlemagne observed. "This is a Dakota fire hole."

Charlemagne brought his hands into the hole.

"It's fresh too," Charlemagne concluded. "How could Tristan have started a fire? He doesn't have any of his supplies? More importantly, if he isn't here, that could only mean…"

Charlemagne frowned.

"He's been kidnapped," Charlemagne thought aloud, bringing his hands to his hair. "Good Lord."

Charlemagne walked over to the beach where Tristan's life vest was. He picked it up and held it. Miklos squatted down to read what was below, pointing at it for Charlemagne to notice. Charlemagne read the message, '*Charles, I am alive and well. I think I've found him. We've set off to return to the ranger station and will see you soon. Please don't worry about us. I'm in good hands. Please trust me – Tristan.*' Charlemagne took a deep breath.

"Have two of your men come to our location," Charlemagne said in a calm voice. "Have them attempt to track Tristan from this location and have another two men go to the nearest warden station to wait for him."

"Yes, Charles," Miklos replied. "What about you?"

"I'm going to return to Diana and let her know that Tristan is alive and well, allegedly…" Charlemagne said. "We're then going back towards the forest fire so that I can disprove Cabernet involvement in the forest fire… have your men provide hourly updates to you about Tristan – I don't want to be kept on the dark on them, either of them."

"Yes, Charles," Miklos nodded. "Of course."

Act 3, Scene 3

Finn and Tristan continued to hike through Leithope Forest, heading south according to Finn's compass. Tristan looked forward as he began to hear the sound of cars passing along a road.

"Are we near a road?" Tristan questioned.

"Probably," Finn replied.

Tristan continued to look forward and saw the motion of a car pass by ahead.

"We are!" Tristan responded.

The two continued to walk and reached the road through the forest. Tristan then looked at either side of the road.

"Which direction?" Tristan questioned.

"Forward," Finn replied.

"What?"

"Are you deaf?"

"No, but I'm not stupid," Tristan said to him. "Isn't it smarter to walk along the edge of the road to get back to civilization?"

"Nah, mate," Finn insisted. "If we do that, we'll be walking for hours. If we cut through, we'll split that time in half. Besides, it's almost nightfall and I'm exhausted – we need to go set up camp."

"Are you serious?" Tristan questioned.

"Trust me," Finn said to him, patting him on the back. "Come on."

Finn and Tristan crossed the road and came to the other side. Tristan looked down one end of the road and then back to Finn who stopped to look at him. He scoffed.

"If you want to carry on by yourself, then by all means," Finn said to him, "but believe me, this is the most efficient route."

Tristan looked at him. He looked at Finn's face and then nodded.

"Stop being such a twat," Finn remarked to him with a smile. "Come on, a couple more minutes and there's a stream up ahead we can camp near."

The two continued downhill from the road and brushed through a dense clearing of shrubs to reach a wide stream. They then followed the stream until they found some ground to set up a camp at. Finn unlatched his backpack and dropped it at the base of a trunk. He then produced a small spade and started to dig into the soil in the center of the camp. He dug two holes and then began to dig a third hole between the two holes.

"Why do you dig fire holes?" Tristan asked. "I mean, I've camped in the mountains in the winter before, and then it made sense to dig into the snow to reach the ground, but why not just make a regular fire pit?"

"It's called a Dakota fire hole," Finn replied. "It makes a hotter fire for less fuel and conceals some of the smoke. It's also easier to cook over since I can just put my grill over the hole and set my pan."

"I'm going to go look for some kindling and tinder," Tristan sighed, leaving.

Tristan returned with some long grass and twigs as well as some sticks. He gave them to Finn who took the grass and wrapped them around almost creating a bird's nest. He then knelt down, took a smooth black rock from his backpack and the knife around his belt. Finn proceeded to streak the edge of the knife over the rock, producing flashes of sparks that landed onto the grass. Tristan took off his pack from around his back and sat down as Finn continued to land sparks into the grass, causing embers to catch onto the grass.

Finn blew some air onto the embers and watched them ignite the grass. He then took the small bunch of grass and lowered it into the hole, feeding twigs until he had a small fire. Finn continued to snap some sticks in half to build the fire. He then took his bucket and grill, placing the grill over the fire and bucket filled with water atop. Finn then started to take out the components to put together his tent, which consisted of two poles, a tarp, and some string. He started with pinning the tent at the four corners and then raised the front, tying a string that stretched forward from the tent and was pegged into the ground. He then raised the back and tied another string to a peg at the back. The tent was small. Finn took out his sleeping bag from his backpack and put it inside the tent. He also took out a blanket.

By the time that Finn had finished, the water started to boil. Finn removed the bucket and separated it from the fire, keeping it aside. He then took out a pan and some leftover fish in plastic bag. He put the fish on the pan and then left the fish over the fire.

The ambience was calm. Tristan and Finn sat in silence as they looked at the fish cooking over the fire. The fire crackled and the two could hear the sound of the stream running not too far from them. The birds were quiet and there was a mild bit of light available as the sun set.

"Do you have any fishing rods?" Tristan asked, breaking the silence.

"No," Finn replied.

"What?"

"No," Finn repeated.

"How are we going to catch fish then?"

Finn shrugged and said, "Same way as last time – don't worry about it. I'll show you tomorrow."

Finn poked at the fillets of fish on the pan. He then turned them before looking at Tristan. He gave a deep breath and looked back at him.

"Who are you?" Finn asked Tristan.

"What?"

"Are you actually deaf?" Finn then asked in an annoyed tone.

"I'm not asking you to repeat the question, I'm questioning the question itself," Tristan clarified. "What kind of vague question is that?"

"A sensible one, I thought," Finn replied. "Who are you?"

Tristan shrugged and then said, "A person."

"Well, that's kind of lame," Finn scoffed. "There are seven billion people in the world. I doubt you're as humble as you want me to think you are."

"Who the hell are you then?" Tristan asked.

Finn took a deep breath and poked at the fish.

"Who do you make me out to be?" Finn asked back, looking at Tristan.

"So, you don't know who you are either?" Tristan instead said to him.

"I know who I am," Finn replied, looking at him, "but it doesn't matter what I say to you, unless you're gullible or naïve enough to really trust my word. Who I am should be based on your perception of what is factual about me, and that is based on your own observations of my actions – not on what I say, or even what other people say."

Finn then looked back at the fire.

"Too many people trust the wrong sources of information when it comes to truth."

Tristan looked at Finn.

"I don't know you well enough to make any judgement of character," Tristan confessed.

"Don't be so modest," Finn scolded. "I'm not asking you to define me or come to some sort of conclusion about me. It's obviously going to be a general and incomplete impression."

Tristan shrugged.

"Fine," Finn sighed, "I see a boy who is unsure of a lot of things. I see someone who probably comes from a rural rather than an urban background to trust a stranger he just met. At the same time, I also see someone who is nice and probably caring about others. He's also someone who's afraid, but at the same time, brave."

"You came up with all that in the less than twenty-four hours we've spent together?" Tristan questioned.

"I'm perceptive," Finn replied.

"So I see," Tristan responded.

"I want to know more about you," Finn asked.

"What do you want to know?"

"What's your ethnicity?"

Tristan shrugged again.

"Canadian?"

Finn sighed and then said, "Let me be more specific. What's your race?"

"White?"

Finn rolled his eyes. He flipped the fish again and then looked back at Tristan.

"Where did your parents come from?" Finn asked this time.

"Okay, I get what you're trying to ask me," Tristan replied, looking back at Finn. "My background is Scottish and Dutch. My dad was the fifth generation of a series of Scottish-Canadians that came to Canada in the 19th century. My mother was the daughter of immigrants that arrived in North Dakota from the Netherlands."

"I guess that makes sense," Finn said, "although your skin tone doesn't make much sense. I suppose it's that Nordic variety that tans really easily. I've seen Norse folk like that before. Red hair is Norse too."

"I'm pretty sure the red hair is just from being Celtic. My dad had auburn hair, and my mother had light brown hair."

"Nah, you're not Celtic, mate," Finn responded. "Believe it or not, but most Scots don't know their own bloody background. They larp as Celts when in reality they're as Anglo as Anglos; Nords, through years of inter-mixing with each other as well as the Viking invasion have made Scotland a Germanic nation. The only true Celts are the Basques, Welsh, and to an extent, the Irish – rural Irish that is."

"What's your ethnicity then?" Tristan questioned in annoyed tone.

"I'm British."

"Is that all?" Tristan asked.

"I'm not a mutt like you," Finn boasted with a smile. "Of course that's all – English to be more specific, of the Nordic variety I suppose, not that there's really a difference unless you're Welsh like I said."

Finn took the fish off of the fire and then served Tristan's portion on a plate, handing it to him with the same titanium fork from lunch. It had been cleaned. The two ate their dinner. Tristan took a bite from the fish. He then cringed as he tasted.

"A little salty…" Tristan said, chewing the fish.

"That's because I cured it in salt," Finn replied. "It's one of the only methods of preserving meat in the wilderness – that and smoking. Literally half of my backpack is filled with packets of salt to preserve meat."

"You just add salt?"

"I cure it in salt, add lots of salt all around the exposed flesh, and it causes water to draw out. Smoking adds a layer of smoke over the meat, which prevents rot. It's really fascinating, given that the mean time for meat to go bad is about two hours."

The two ate and then Finn took Tristan's plate and the pan and went to wash them in the stream before returning to the camp. Tristan stayed near the fire as it had grown dark.

Finn took his water bottle from his backpack, filled it with the water in the bucket that had been boiled, and then placed it back in his backpack. He then took a steel mug and poured a glass of water, handing it to Tristan.

"Drink up," Finn said, "we're going to have to share a bottle until we set up another camp."

"How far are we from the station?" Tristan questioned with skeptical eyes on Finn.

"Dunno," Finn responded, "probably another day's hike – can never be too sure. I want to stock up on some food before we set off again tomorrow though in case I'm wrong."

"Don't you have a map?" Tristan asked.

"Yeah, but don't worry about it," Finn replied.

Tristan looked at him with the mug in hand.

"What's really going on here?" Tristan questioned.

"Nothing," Finn insisted. "I'm getting you home – are you in a hurry?"

"I- I mean, not really, but…"

"Then stop complaining," Finn replied. "I'll get you back to your folks soon enough. I'm just being careful."

"You don't seem like someone to be careful – otherwise you wouldn't be out here on your own," Tristan responded. "You'd be out here with friends or something."

"I… I don't really have any friends," Finn said in a saddened tone. "There's not a lot of people who behave and act like me." Tristan looked at Finn and then looked away.

"I'm sorry," Tristan responded.

The two went quiet for a moment. Finn took the bucket and went back to the stream. He then returned and sat down across from Tristan. Tristan looked to him. He cleared this throat.

"If it makes you feel any better," Tristan said, "I don't really have any friends back home either."

Finn didn't reply. He instead took some sticks and fed them into the fire.

"I'm going to bed," Finn said. "There's enough room for the two of us in the tent, but keep to yourself, okay?"

"Sure," Tristan responded.

Finn took off his shirt as if it were a jacket and brought it over his backpack. He then knelt down in front of the tent and took his sleeping bag. He opened it and unzipped the side, folding the bag out and laying it inside the tent as if it were a mattress. He then climbed into the tent and lay down so that his head was facing out. Tristan looked at the fire for another minute and then over to Finn as he stretched out a blanket.

"Thanks for sharing and looking out for me," Tristan said to Finn. "It's nice of you – you're nice."

"No, I'm not," Finn responded, lying on his side. "I'm just looking out for my common blood."

Tristan looked at Finn and then shook his head.

Act 3, Scene 4

At noon the next day, Tristan watched Finn as he walked carefully around in the water of the stream near their camp, which was more of a river than a creek, but at the crossroad of the two in terms of definition. He had constructed a trap early in the morning out of the rocks and a large log in the stream to lure fish and entrap them. The entrance of the trap was pointed upstream so that fish climbing upwards would unintentionally be caught in as they were redirected by the log, acting as an obstruction, which pointed into the pool surrounded by large rocks. The sun was gazing down hard and Finn was concentrating on the fish in the water – the fish was medium-sized and swimming between the many circular atriums of the maze that Finn had made.

Finn had blocked the exit off and was carefully chasing the fish in an attempt to grab it. He lurched his hands into the water and grabbed the fish by its sides, holding on tight as he pulled it out of the water and raised it out. The fish flailed around. Tristan stood up as Finn returned with the fish, walking back onto the land with the fish barefoot and bringing it to the ground. Finn hit the fish in the head and knocked it out. He then took his knife and inserted it into the back of the fish's head.

"There you go – that's lunch and dinner for us," Finn said, picking up the fish and showing it to Tristan with a proud smile.

"Congratulations," Tristan responded in a sarcastic tone. "I'm starving…"

"Take this lad back to the camp for me while I wash up before lunch – feel free to fillet it before I get back," Finn said, handing him the fish in one hand and knife in the other.

Tristan took back and then left to return to the camp. He brought the fish to a cutting board near the campfire and brought it atop. He then knelt down in front of it and looked at the fish with a frustrated face. The dead fish looked back at him through its dead eye.

"I don't even know how to fillet a fish…" Tristan muttered, leaning back.

Tristan left the knife next to the fish and backed off, inching back to rest his back against a log as he looked at the fish with spite. Finn returned soon enough, dressed and with a towel in hand. He brought the towel to the clothes line in a spot of sun and then looked to Tristan and the fish.

"I see you've filleted the fish," Finn sarcastically said, kneeling down and spinning the board around so that it could face him. "You could have in the least gutted it."

Finn took the knife and slit the fish under the stomach. He then put his hands inside and took out the guts, leaving them on the board. Once he was done, Finn brought the blade into the gills of the fish by the neck as he held his other hand at the head. He cut through, but did not go all the way. He instead kept the knife inside and turned it to cut through the ribs towards the tail. He then turned the fish around and finished cutting away from the backbone so he could strip the piece of meat off. The meat was rubber-like and slippery. His hands had grown bloody. He left the fillet above the fish as he turned it onto the opposite side to do the same. Once he was done, nothing was left of the original fish but the head and tail attached via the spine. Finn took it and held it for Tristan.

"Go on and get rid of that for me," Finn said, preferably towards the stream and not the latrine hole.

"Sure," Tristan replied, taking the fish back to the stream and laying it in the water.

Tristan then returned as Finn removed the ribs from the fish and brought pieces onto the pan to cook. He then took a transparent plastic bag from the other night, cleaned, and left some small pieces inside.

"Hopefully we can get another fish – or else this'll be a lame supper," Finn said, looking at the meat in the bag and then back to Tristan.

"Alternatively, we could eat at the warden station you're planning to take me to," Tristan replied to him. "Like you said you would."

"You want me to go to the warden station? I'll take you there – I'm going to keep that promise," Finn responded, "but I'm not leaving the forest, or compromising myself either. The fish'll be my supper."

"Why?"

"Because I caught it…"

"No, why won't you want to leave? There's a forest fire raging up north and you want to stay?" Tristan questioned. "You didn't get separated from your troops by accident, did you? You purposefully separated yourself from them because you wanted to be alone."

"Yes, I wanted to be alone," Finn responded, looking at him, "and at the same time, you think I want to keep you around. How contradictory. I came here to get away from the city, and I'm not going back," he added in a sharp tone. "I don't care if there's a fire, I'm moving south away from the fire anyways. I know what I'm doing, so shut up."

Finn served one of the fishes on the pan onto a plate and then handed it to Tristan.

"Now eat your bloody fish and keep your mouth shut," Finn remarked, crossing his arms. "You look prettier that way."

• • •

Once the two had eaten, Finn packed up the camp and the two set off back to the road, following it until they came to a large house at the edge of the street. A sign outside of the house read, 'Whitelee Warden Station.' Finn took Tristan to the gates going towards the causeway that wrapped around the front lawn of the station.

A sign attached to the gate read to them, *'Closed due to Wildfire'* alongside a list of phone numbers below and a website. Finn sighed and then looked to Tristan.

"Sorry," Finn said to him.

Tristan looked back at him. He then looked at the sign and then down to the ground.

"It's not your fault," Tristan replied.

"Come on – come with me," Finn insisted. "I'm going down south away from the fire, and…"

"And?" Tristan questioned.

"I don't mind you sticking with me," Finn responded. "It's nice to have someone around who isn't a total idiot."

"Thanks…" Tristan replied, "but my guardian is going to get worried if I don't get into contact with him."

"We'll set off for the station on the opposite-end," Finn suggested. "I doubt they'll be closed if the fire is in the north."

"Okay…" Tristan replied, "let's go then."

Tristan and Finn left the gate of the warden station and then went back to the road. Tristan stopped as he looked to the side and saw an SUV drive down the road. He paused for a moment as Finn continued to walk across the road after the car had left. Tristan looked to the opposite side and then to the back of Finn. He took his watch from its strap and then went to the gate, leaving the watch there before rushing back to Finn. Finn looked at him, but the two didn't say anything as they journeyed back into the forest, entering Tarset Forest once more.

Act 3, Scene 5

Tristan and Finn laid down on the dirt of the forest around them, looking up to the sky past the trees above. Two days had passed since they had arrived at the Whitelee Warden Station and the sun was stinging down hard on them – it was over thirty degrees Celsius, and they were still in Tarset Forest, moving less than a couple kilometers per evening due to the heat. They were in a dirt clearing with pieces of wood and rocks around them.

The pair kept their eyes up, listening to the sounds around them with steady breaths. Each of them had their feet pointed at opposite directions, but their heads side by side, right ear to right ear. Finn was dressed in similar clothes to two days prior but washed. He had taken off his tank top due to the heat and only wore the scout shirt with the buttons undone and sleeves rolled up. Tristan wore his original shorts, slightly wrinkled, and no shirt. Neither of them had their shoes on.

"I'm not feeling anything," Tristan said, letting out a deep exhale.

"Shut up," Finn responded in a calm voice. "If you keep talking, you won't feel anything. Just keep looking up and concentrate on something other than yourself. Just… embrace your surroundings and take deep breaths."

Finn and Tristan both took slow, but deep breaths. They continued to lay on the ground alone for another couple of minutes. Finn closed his eyes for most of them. Tristan laid there and listened to the ambience of birds chirping, leaves rustling and the distant movement of water in the lake near their camp not too far. Tristan closed his eyes and then opened them again to look upwards at the tips of the deciduous trees mixed with coniferous. The trees were tall and stretched out towards the clear blue ceiling.

Another ten minutes passed and then another ten minutes as they continued to lie in the middle of the forest together. Finn opened his eyes and held a light smile on his face.

"Isn't this nice?" Finn questioned.

"I wish I was enjoying this as much as you," Tristan confessed, sighing.

"You're not enjoying it because you don't know what it is that we're supposed to be enjoying," Finn replied to him. "Focus on your senses and see, listen at all that is around us – it is the beauty of nature and there is none like it anywhere else. Tristan, this is our land – the land of our people, the land of our ancestors – it is our home. The trees around us have known our people for more centuries, the wilderness around us has nourished and given us the strengths to survive and live on. The culture of our people was born out of the forest…"

Tristan continued to look up as Finn paused.

"Man is one with the Eternal One in this forest – man is in contact with Him in this forest because He is the beautiful and the sublime."

Tristan did not respond. Finn sat up and turned back to Tristan. Tristan pointed his eyes up as he noticed Finn sit up. He then did the same and turned around. Finn turned and brought himself closer to Tristan so that they were sat next to each other.

"Please, tell me that you feel what I feel," Finn encouraged, "the happiness of being in this forest and being as we are. We are in our native lands where violence and bloodshed led to the creation of men and culture. All that is ours can be pointed back to the forest – we are a forest people."

Tristan looked at Finn with intent, seeing his diluted blue eyes and looking at him with slight pity, or perhaps, self-pity. Finn took Tristan's right hand.

"Bring your hand into the dirt," Finn said to him, scooping their hands together into the dirt. "This is the dirt of your ancestors, of our ancestors – our blood is tied to this soil. The blood of soldiers and warriors, conquerors, and knights, nourished by this soil and to this soil do we owe our gratitude and love. We have a duty to protect this forest from those that threaten it – we have a duty to protect our people, our family, our common blood, because they are all we have. One protects what they love… and there is nothing wrong in loving one's own ancestral land and people."

Finn took a deep breath.

"Why would one want to throw away something as precious as blood for frivolous and pitiful endeavors and spoils?" Finn questioned him. "Even in this day, soldiers are needed to defend against the demons of greed and lust, but men of principle are lacking. Don't you want to be a warrior, Tristan? To fight for what is good and defend what you love? It is the ultimate expression of manhood to fight the dragon, Tristan. You must fight the dragon."

Finn hit Tristan in the chest with the back of his hand. He then stood up with a smile.

"Be like Saint George and slay the dragon who thirsts on our blood," Finn encouraged, grabbing a long stick from the ground. "The dragon of Moloch awaits to be slain and we are in short supply of good men to do so."

Finn picked up another stick and tossed one to Tristan. Tristan caught it with both hands and the blocked Finn's swipe towards him, pushing him back and then standing up. Finn held a smile as he took another swipe towards Tristan, pretending the sticks to be swords, Tristan grew a smile and played with him.

"There are many evils in our modern world," Finn stated to Tristan as they sparred, "and our people, our homes, and our livelihood are under threat."

Tristan took a swipe towards Finn. Finn backed up his stomach as the stick narrowly passed him. He then whacked the stick towards Tristan, but Tristan blocked with his own. The two then struggled as Finn pushed himself towards Tristan.

"Don't you agree with anything I've said?" Finn questioned.

Tristan didn't respond. The two simply looked at each other as Finn continued to press himself forward. Finn looked at Tristan's green eyes and eased his tension.

"You do agree... you're just scared to admit it because of what it means..." Finn said. "You need to be brave!"

Tristan kicked Finn back with his foot. Finn brought his stick to Tristan's side, but Tristan blocked it and the brought his own stick up, grazing Finn at the left cheek and causing him to bring his hand up to it.

"Oh crap!" Tristan reacted, eyes widening. "I didn't mean to hurt you!"

Tristan threw his sword onto the ground and then rushed over to Finn. Finn held a smile and punched Tristan in the shoulder, marking Tristan's right shoulder with his blood.

"You didn't hurt me," Finn remarked to him. "I wouldn't even say you've injured me – this is superficial."

"Do you have a first aid kit? I'll help you disinfect and patch it up to avoid an infection," Tristan suggested.

"Yeah, but don't worry about it," Finn responded. "I can go and get it myself – I'm fine."

"Just stay here," Tristan insisted, "and keep pressure on that wound."

Tristan rushed off.

"Tristan!" Finn shouted to him.

Tristan ignored him and returned to the camp. He went to Finn's backpack and began to rummage through his things, reaching the bottom where the first aid kit was. He picked the first aid kit out and heard Finn arriving behind him. Tristan looked at the very bottom of Finn's backpack and saw a curious transparent package of a sort of white clay substance. He placed his hands inside and took the item out, reading the label and dropping it in shock and horror. The packet read on the front in black print, '*Block, Demolition, M4*' and then below, '*C4 Explosive.*'

Finn grabbed the package before it rolled towards the fire pit and then took his backpack. He took both and walked at least two meters from Tristan to put the items back inside. Tristan looked at the back of Finn with wide eyes. Finn lowered the backpack by a tree.

"Why do you have C4 explosives?!" Tristan questioned him in a low voice as if someone else were near. "Why – what the hell man?!"

"Shut up!" Finn responded, going over to him and placing a hand over his mouth.

Tristan pushed him back.

"Please, just keep your cool," Finn pleaded. "It's not what it looks like…"

"Oh, I suppose those are casually just for camping then – you know, in case you need to blow something up for the sake of survival."

"It's not like that, please," Finn remarked. "Please, Tristan, let me explain myself."

Tristan did not respond.

"I'm not a boy scout…" Finn confessed. "I came to this forest on my own after I heard about the forest fire. I needed an insert, so I lied about being a boy scout… it was a small lie, and

I'm sorry I lied to you, but I really am who I said I am from there on. You see, my father is the owner of a large multi-billion dollar empire, and I know it was him and his people who started the forest fire above. My intentions in being here have been to seek revenge against him, because this forest *is* the home our ancestors and I will defend it whatever the cost."

"You're insane," Tristan simply said, shaking his head. "You're actually insane."

"No, don't say that," Finn denied, waving a finger at Tristan. "You heard me back over there – you listened to what I was saying, and although you didn't say you agreed, I saw in your eyes that you knew I was right."

"Violence is never the answer," Tristan replied, "even if this is our home, our people, whatever – violence is never the answer to a violent problem. You can fight your father by other means, if he's even responsible for what you say he is responsible for…"

"He is."

"There are other means, please, Finn," Tristan pleaded. "Do not throw your life away from something as insignificant as them – you can do a lot more damage if you are patient."

"I'm sorry," Finn replied, "but there is no political solution. We are at war."

Tristan shook his head and looked at Finn with hurtful eyes. He then turned his back to him.

"Join me," Finn requested. "We can do good together, I know we can."

"No," Tristan quietly replied, bringing a hand to his forehead. "I'm sorry, but I don't see eye-to-eye with you. I…"

"Are you going to leave me?" Finn questioned. "Abandon me? Report me?"

"I…" Tristan responded, hesitating to respond. "I… I can't abandon you – no, because I know that you know, that this is just not right…"

Tristan turned around and looked to him.

"I want to help you, Finn, but not like this – what was even your plan?"

Finn paused as he looked to the ground and then to Tristan.

"There is a natural gas facility south of here across the Scottish border owned by my father," Finn explained. "The plant rings in millions in profit to my father's organization and if I were to set off this bomb, it would do massive damage to his operations that would offset the cost of the fire."

Tristan sighed.

"Are you coming with me then?" Finn questioned.

"I… Please, Finn, there's more that we can do to expose your father if he is guilty. We can prove he is guilty…"

"He *is* guilty."

"The world doesn't work that way though," Tristan complained. "It's not a sensible system. It's a system of laws and procedures – it doesn't care if the objective truth is that your father is guilty, but if the courts can be persuaded through plausible evidence…"

"In other words, the courts are flawed and therefore it's hopeless to believe that they can do anything," Finn replied, crossing his arms. "You know I'm right."

Tristan frowned. He crossed his own arms.

"I'll only help you if you promise to me that you'll seek non-violent methods," Tristan proposed, "but you have to promise. I'll go with you to this plant – we'll sleuth around, but that is all we'll do. There'll be no sabotage."

Finn looked to Tristan with sharp eyes. He then gave a deep sigh and uncrossed his arms.

"Fine, but only because I think it'll be a learning experience for you to realize how right I am, and how wrong you really are." The two shook hands.

Act 4, Scene 1

Charlemagne looked at Tristan's watch as he rode in the front of an armored car driving back to Otterburn along the A68. The morning skies were obscured with smoke, hazy and polluted like a grey day. The smoke caused the daylight to be slightly dim as well. On the right-side of the road, various vehicles were parked including fire engines, supply trucks, and other vehicles as part of the firefighting effort. Charlemagne fiddled with the watch and then hid it in the inner pocket of his camouflaged jacket.

"I heard from Lukas before we left," Miklos said, focusing on the road. "He said he's following Tristan and this unknown boy in Tarset. They're at least a day behind them but are keeping up. He's safe."

"I know he'd be safe... it doesn't mean I'm not bothered with worry anyways," Charlemagne responded, looking into the side-view mirror and at Diana in the back.

The car continued to drive forward back along the road. The second car was behind them. Diana held a sunken face as she looked out of the car and towards the forest. She could see glimmers of fire beyond the trees. Miklos had the air conditioning turned on in the car, making it extremely cool. Diana wore a coat to overcome the chill.

At the end of the A68 was a checkpoint that brought them out of the forest. The car drove for another couple of meters to reach the manor house of the warden station. The large acre of land that surrounded the warden station had become occupied by additional vehicles that were part of the firefighting effort as well as large white tents. A makeshift helicopter landing pad had been added as well. The light helicopter belonging to the Protection Squad was parked on the grass near the lodge. The armored cars drove up the causeway outside of the lodge and parked outside. Miklos then turned off the car engine and exited the vehicle. Charlemagne and Diana followed and they came into the inside of the house.

Miklos took a pass from his jacket and brought it to a card reader near the glass door going into the private space of the station.

"Stay here with Diana," Charlemagne told Hardrada and Holger. "Better yet, take her to a room upstairs. We have two reserved for us, well, the kids."

"Yes, Mr. Cabernet," Hardrada responded, leading Diana into the private area of the house.

The two groups then separated. Charlemagne walked with Igor and Miklos to the left while the others went to the right. Charlemagne then turned into a corridor that led towards the war room. There were a lot more people in the room than when Charlemagne arrived and the room had become crowded.

Telephones rang and just about every available warden was in the room with them, on phones and speaking with someone somewhere. The head warden was at the map in the center of the room, looking at the current situation of the fire. Charlemagne went over and stood across from him. The former tokens that were being used to represent the area of the fire had been abandoned in favor of crossed lines marked into the map with a thick red marker denoting ravaged land. A certain portion of the forest, in the north at Hethpool, was marked in black. The forest behind the ranger station, was unaffected due to a line at the border of the forest between Otterburn Forest and the southeast of Barrow Burn.

"Where the hell have you been? You've been gone for almost three days before we heard from you!" the head warden complained. "Never mind, the situation is dire, more dire than it previously was – due to unfortunate winds to the west, the fire broke through our line at the A68 and pushed into the center of the park. It's inserted itself into Tarset and is going south. I've petitioned fire retardant to be airdropped towards here," he said, pointing at the freeway that divided the center of the park with the southern sector. "We've had crews developing various fire lines all around, but the breadth of the forest makes it difficult to cover the entire sector. Hopefully, we should stop the fire from reaching Kielder for a day or two."

"My people will ensure that funds are allocated to pay for the fire retardant drops," Charlemagne stated. "I know that they are expensive, but it is my belief that they are necessary."

"Thank you," the head warden said, taking a sigh of relief. "You have no idea how thankful we are for your aid – it's some of the biggest we've received apart from the foreign help."

Charlemagne nodded. The head warden was interrupted and spoken to by a man next to him. The two bickered and whispered to each other. The head warden then looked back to Charlemagne.

"We have another task for you," the head warden said, receiving a folder. "A group of scientists from the University of Oxford appear to be under threat of being surrounded in the north of the forest, near one of the fire lines here."

The head warden pointed to the middle of the north section, to Hethpool and at a bulge in the frontline.

"Although some of these spots have started to extinguish with our volleys of water, this team managed to get themselves stuck in a hard place," the warden explained. "I need your team to fly over and help them get out safely."

"Understood," Charlemagne responded, looking at the map.

Miklos took the folder and began to take note of the location with Igor.

"We'll set off immediately," Charlemagne added, helping the others with coordinates.

· · ·

Charlemagne boarded the light helicopter with Miklos and Igor, and the light helicopter then set off north towards Otterburn Forest. All of the team except Charlemagne was equipped with oxygen tanks at their backs and helmets. Charlemagne sat in the cockpit with a pair of sunglasses on as they travelled towards the fire with smoke pluming out of the forest in the distance. The helicopter travelled to the large plume of smoke and went above the clouds rising from the forest. Charlemagne attempted to look down, towards the fire below, but was blinded by the white smoke.

The helicopter came through to the other side after making its long journey, arriving over Leithope before going northward towards Butterburn. Butterburn was distinct with the fields and farmland below. The helicopter stayed on course by following the border between this farmland and the forest on the east, eventually arriving towards their destination and setting down through the smoke and entering a dark and dismal place that was the bulge on the frontline. Overall, the journey from Otterburn to the landing site was less than ten minutes.

Charlemagne looked ahead and could see the fires rampaging ahead, consuming the forest with its dancing flames. For now, it appeared as though the fire was stagnant and the lines were holding. The skies above were not white, but grey with the brightness of the fire creating an orange-grey apocalyptic appearance. The helicopter touched down in the small, hilly clearing which had tall grass. Not too far from the landing site was a small camp with white tents and a recreational vehicle parked. Charlemagne could see people moving around at the side.

"Stay here," Charlemagne told the pilot. "We have four scientists returning with us."

"Yes, Mr. Cabernet," the pilot responded.

Charlemagne exited the cockpit and went off with Miklos and Igor as they went towards the campsite. Miklos led the team and faced the scientists.

"Excuse me, but it is time for you all to leave," Miklos shouted. "We have orders from the Department of the Environment, Farmland, and Rural Affairs, to have you evacuated due to risk of becoming entrapped in the wildfire."

"No way," a man said in a Liverpool accent.

The man had long brown hair and brown eyes. He also had round sunglasses and fair skin. He wore a denim jacket and khaki shorts.

"We were permitted to document the wildfire for research purposes," the man explained. "How can we be forced out?"

"I'm sorry, but that is what we have been ordered to assist with, so if you could please come with us, we will assist you out," Miklos replied.

"Can we at least pack our equipment?" the man questioned. "We have thousands of dollars of expensive equipment lying around here!"

"There is no time," Charlemagne interjected, "I'm sorry, but your lives are worth more than the material goods here. The bushfire is on its approach towards your camp and there will be no means of escape for you and your team. Either you come with us, or we will have to physically assist you."

The man shook his head, slammed a pencil onto the ground, and then brought his hands up in defeat.

"Fine!" the man submitted.

Charlemagne stood-by as the man came over to them. He was accompanied by two females. Charlemagne counted them with his eyes and then looked to Miklos.

"Where's the fourth?" Charlemagne questioned to him.

An older woman with blonde hair turned back and looked out to the camp.

"Arnold!" the woman shouted, looking to Charlemagne. "I last saw him near the creek..."

"Stay with the others," Charlemagne told the woman, pointing her towards the helicopter. "We'll look for him."

Charlemagne looked towards Igor.

"Get these people out of here at once!" Charlemagne shouted. "We'll look for the missing person!"

"Yes, sir!" Igor replied.

Charlemagne and Miklos set off past the camp and towards the edge of the forest. They came to a deep creek at the edge of the forest, below a ridge and looked around. Charlemagne stared ahead to the forest. The fire

"We're finally here, near where the fire started," Charlemagne said to Miklos.

"You're not seriously considering..."

"Charlie-One, we've located Dr. Watts – what's your location?" Igor communicated over the radio. "We've received word that the fire has broken through – we've got less than a minute or two until this entire area is decimated."

Miklos looked to Charlemagne. Charlemagne looked back at him and then behind as he noticed a terrible crackle of the conflagration on its approach to them.

"Charlie-Six, this is Charlie Actual," Charlemagne replied. "There's no time. Set off with the goods and we'll await your return when it is safe."

"Are you certain?" Igor questioned.

"I'm certain. Leave immediately."

Charlemagne looked back towards the firestorm as it closed in on them. Miklos quickly grabbed Charlemagne by his waist and the two plunged into the water below. Charlemagne opened his eyes and looked above him as hell let loose and the self-propelled wind of fire swept through the land. The two of them stayed submerged until the flames above settled down. Afterwards, Charlemagne rose to the surface and looked around them as they found themselves in the midst of the forest fire.

Act 4, Scene 2

Finn got down on one knee and brought his hand to the ground before him. Tristan stood behind him as he looked at the markings on the ground. The markings had an appearance of two oblongs in the shape of tears. The points of the markings pointed forward. Finn stood up and looked ahead. He then pointed Tristan to go ahead.

Finn was dressed in a black baseball cap and green-black flannel shirt with the buttons open and sleeves rolled up. Underneath he had his white tank top. He also wore beige shorts. Tristan wore the change of clothes that Finn had given him – the t-shirt and shorts.

Tristan held onto the longbow and a bag of arrows. He followed Finn from behind as he led him further along the Tarset Forest with careful steps. They walked for a couple of minutes in total silence to one another until Finn stopped Tristan and froze completely. He stepped down and looked ahead, hitting Tristan in the chest and then pointing to what he saw. Tristan looked, squinting ahead.

In the slight distance, with a great breadth of antlers, was a male-deer, a stag, looking to the side. The deer turned its gaze towards the boys and then ran off. Finn continued on forward and the two treaded carefully as they came to some pushes by the water. Finn knelt down behind the bush. Tristan joined him and looked down to the stag by the water in the gulley below. Finn pulled at Tristan's shirt and dragged him next to him.

Finn looked to Tristan with a shy smile with his face at least an inch to his.

"Just like we talked about," Finn whispered to him. "Aim for the vitals above the forelimb, but behind the shoulder."

Tristan nodded and drew an arrow. He prepared his bow and aimed at the stag as it continued to drink. Finn peaked over the bush to watch. Tristan held onto the bow with a mild tremble. He drew the arrow back but held on for over a minute. Finn looked over to him. Tristan released.

The sound of the arrow firing caused the stag to look up and over to him. The arrow hit the deer in the side, causing him to shout in pain and rear from his hind legs. Finn cheered.

"Nice!" Finn shouted.

The stag ran off and went up the gulley, into the forest ahead. Tristan lowered the bow and stared ahead while Finn stood up and began to cut through the bush to get below to the gulley. He looked at Tristan and pushed him at the forearm.

"Let's go!" Finn said to him. "We've got to get 'im before he hides on us."

"Yeah," Tristan replied, nodding and following him.

The boys crossed the creek and climbed over the ridge to the other side of the forest. From there, Finn examined the ground in search of stains of blood from the bleeding out stag. The two then went into the forest. Finn walked carefully, keeping his eyes on the ground while Tristan simply walked behind him with a saddened look on his face. Finn looked to him.

"What the hell is wrong with you?" Finn questioned.

Tristan sighed and said, "Nothing."

"Don't be a faggot," Finn responded. "I see you're upset. I also saw that you hesitated to take that shot – I knew you would hesitate, which is why I made you do it. You were afraid to take the life of another living being."

Tristan rolled his eyes.

"Your compassion is a weakness that would only lead to your demise if you didn't live in a cushioned society," Finn remarked to him. "It's people like you who aren't raised properly to see the adverse situation of the world – who sees these animals as fluffy and cute, and not as the soulless beings they are. The peace and comfort of our society is a temporary luxury against the natural violence and strife."

"You're a sociopath," Tristan simply replied.

Finn stopped in the midst of his tracking and turned to Tristan, walking towards him.

"Do you not think that this deer had some sort of innocence towards him?" Finn questioned, pointing his fingers at Tristan's chest. "Are you not this naïve? For all we know, that deer was making its way raping does, or other stags for that matter – all it did was eat and crap as it pleased. What a life? It was a beast – all animals are beasts. Do you know what else? Humans are not any more special than him. Do you think that because we can talk to one another, we invent, create, and live in 'civilized societies,' we're special? No, we're no different than them. We're animals tormented with some strange disorder in our brains… mine has sent me to wander alone."

"We're not animals," Tristan responded. "I mean, phylogenetically speaking, we are, but we are also more. Our essence isn't a disorder. We have principles. We have morals. We have laws…"

"Laws…" Finn questioned under his breath, speaking up to say, "Laws are man-made rules, and I have nothing but contempt for man and his rules."

Tristan looked back at Finn. He looked at the scab on his face from yesterday, under his left eye.

"So, you love your people, but you also hate them. Do you hate me?"

"No," Finn responded, "and it's not like that – you don't understand."

Finn sighed.

"I do care about people – my foremost concern if the wellbeing of my people and their future, but a worthwhile future. I hold contempt for the modern man because he does not care about himself. He indulges in self-gratification and meaningless pleasures. We live in a utilitarian society – do you know what that means? It is a society where the primary concern of the people, of government, and of society is how they can achieve the maximum amount of happiness, and this type of society is unfortunately also a materialistic one that seeks to achieve happiness through materialistic means – consumer goods, and at heart, money. By no means are material things and happiness evil or wrong, but they are not the path to happiness. We live in the most depressed society – even peasants of the medieval era had a better life than the modern working class. Women have not been liberated. They have been enslaved. The family has not been made better, it has been destroyed. Our societies have not been enriched by third-world immigration, it has been *polluted*. All of these calamities have one definite rootless root, but you're not ready to hear that yet..."

Finn gave a long sigh as he looked to Tristan.

"If I didn't care, I wouldn't put in all this effort..." Finn said to him. "You don't understand – you're young and I was where you are once. I didn't understand. I was lost and hopeless. I was probably worse off, but then again, maybe you are worse off."

Finn sighed once more. He turned around from Tristan.

"Most people think the rich don't suffer, but we do – some of us, a very small portion. I had an empty life without parents – not that I consider those frauds to be my actual parents. I hate them. It's because of them, I've lived a sheltered life. It's because of them I've had to suffer, and suffer I have. Life is hard... for four years I've had to come to understand that, and when I finally did come to understand, I was set free. The truth set me free over the mainstream idea that suffering can somehow be eliminated? Evaded? Cured? No. Suffering is not bad – all men should have to suffer, and to get through that suffering, one has to soldier on and fight. Life is not about the victory at the end, it's about the battle. If life were about the victory, all life would be tragic because we all die in the end – a wise man said that. Only those that are willing to fight for their life deserve to live. Only those, if they hold the willpower necessary to overcome their adversity, deserve to be on this blessed Earth."

Finn stretched out his arms and took a deep breath.

"The world is beautiful and that beauty and its truth is what keeps me on this straight path – to know that we are not alone and there is a God out there," Finn remarked, lowering his hands. "I don't consider that deer to be unclean even if it is an inferior creature – the inferior are never by default unclean or unholy. I am inferior to God – why is that a problem? No, I see that deer as a beautiful creature and all of man as beautiful people who have sadly been led astray. Do you understand that?"

Finn turned to Tristan. Tristan simply looked awkwardly to him. Finn held a sunken look on his face as if he had just ran a mile. He was panting slightly. His cheeks were red. Tristan walked over to him.

"Come on, that deer's probably bled out by now – let's go find him," Tristan said in a weak voice, passing him.

Finn looked back to Tristan with a frown. He nodded and the two walked together through the rest of the forest as they came to the end, reaching a grass field of a downwards hill that led to a fence. Behind the fence was a grain field with a barn and farmhouse nearby. The farm was bordered by a line of deciduous trees, with a power line in front, and behind the trees was another farmhouse hidden behind. In the background were rolling grass hills with neat groups of trees. Finn looked at the tracks below in the dirt and the two continued down the hill to come to the fence.

"Looks like he hopped over this fence and went into the farm," Finn told Tristan. "Come on."

Finn vaulted over the fence and came to the other side. Tristan joined him and the two began to cross the grain field as Finn observed markings of blood in the tall green wheat. Tristan kept his eyes out and scanned the area as they walked. To the side of the field they crossed was a croft with sheep. The two were alone in the immediate area with no other humans in sight.

At the end of the field were some tracks in the dirt that led towards the barn. Tristan observed that the barn door was open wide. The two entered and saw their stag passed out in a pool of its own blood at the side of the fence of a horse. Tristan looked at the dead deer with an upset face while Finn went over to pull it away from the fence by its legs.

"Give me a hand here," Finn said to Tristan.

Tristan went over and took the hind legs. The two then pulled the deer out.

"No way we're getting this lad out of here," Finn complained, removing his arrow from the animal's body. "We'll just have to take the easiest part out here and take it to cook back in the forest. With this weather, we have less than two hours before the whole thing is spoiled."

Finn took his knife and then looked to Tristan.

"You might want to look away if this interferes with your precious morals," Finn remarked to Tristan with a hint of sarcasm.

"Shut up," Tristan replied, frowning at him.

Finn took his large knife and brought it to the hind leg, towards the knee. He then made an incision and proceeded to attempt to snap the leg off, twisting it until it detached. Tristan cringed at the sound of the bone snapping. Finn tossed aside the lower limb and then did the same to the other hind leg.

"H-have you done this before?" Tristan questioned.

"Yeah..." Finn replied. "At least once. I'm not going to skin the whole thing, just these legs – I don't even have time to gut it."

Finn took his knife and grabbed the thigh of the stag. He inserted his knife into the meat, made an incision outwards before inserting the tip into the thigh, behind the hide, and then pushing inwards before pushing out. The hide of the deer at the thigh pulled apart, exposing a white membrane known as silver skin. Finn then pulled the fur back and pushed his knife in, carving the hide and leaving behind the skin. He did the same to the other side and then continued, drawing the fur back to the buttocks. He then made another incision at the midline and pulled down, avoiding to cut into the inner organs as he focused on skinning the deer. He cut down to the center of the deer and then returned upwards to push his knife in and tear the fur from the silver skin. Once enough of the fur had been pulled, he was about to tear it off with his hands at either side before pulling down and leaving behind a skinned deer up to his midline incision.

"Look at that – that is meat!" Finn cheered, slapping the top of the thigh and looking to Tristan. "Now it gets a little messier..."

Tristan looked at him unimpressed. Finn grabbed the thigh by the leg and stepped around to stand behind the deer. He then pulled the thigh back and inserted his knife into pelvis of the deer, cutting down to separate the muscle from the hip. He then ran the knife again and came against the socket. Finn became more aggressive as he attempted to detach the socket from the shank, pulling to get it loose.

The shank tore off. Finn stood up and held the shank in his hands, looking to Tristan.

"I forgot they always look bigger after you cut," Finn remarked, looking to Tristan. "I don't think we'll need more than one."

"So, we're just going to leave it here for the owners to come and find?" Tristan questioned as Finn started to leave.

"Do you want to carry it out with me? Risk getting caught? No? Then shut up and let's go," Finn responded. "Come on."

• • •

Finn cooked the thigh, cutting it into smaller pieces once they had a fire started not too far from the farm. Tristan separated the bow string from the bow as the meat cooked. Once it was ready, they ate and then proceeded to leave again, walking along the sides of the forest to avoid the farm they had trespassed through. The two came back out of the forest and reached a small, narrow country road that they began to walk along.

"We're less than a day away from the plant," Finn told Tristan, looking at his map. "We can make another camp out in the bushes again once the sun sets."

Tristan nodded and looked back to Finn. The two continued to walk together in silence for another few minutes until Tristan looked to Finn once more.

"What are your dreams?" Tristan asked Finn. "What do you want to achieve in life?"

"To secure the existence and reproduction of my race and people, and a future for our children where they can thrive, be healthy, free and independent," Finn replied.

"You want to have kids?" Tristan then asked.

"I like kids," Finn responded. "A lot of the reason why I'm doing this is to safeguard a better future for the children, but I don't think I'll get to have them."

"Why?" Tristan questioned.

Finn shrugged.

"Okay," Tristan replied, "but what about before you believed all of this? What did you want to do when you were a kid? What did you look at and aspire to be when you grew up?"

"Honestly, when I was at least six or seven, I wanted to be a scientist, well – to be more accurate, an aerospace engineer making jets. I thought that would be the coolest thing back in the day, but it didn't last – I mean, I guess it still would be cool. I wasn't that terrible of a student and did pretty well in physics and maths to get into a good university, but... I don't see any point in doing so. I had a romanticized vision when I was growing up of being able to settle down, hold a steady job and have a family of my own – a middle-class family, not upper class in some sort of suburbs, and perhaps in America. Whatever I did didn't really interest me that much as long as I had that family. When I was in grammar school, I was divided on what I should set myself off to study. I liked science and maths, but I also enjoyed history and English. I felt like I could never find a common ground between them and that I was in equal skill in all of them to decide what I should focus on more. Even now, I think I'm just average in all of them to really specialize. I have no idea what to do with my life. What about you?"

"I've wanted to be a doctor since I was thirteen," Tristan replied. "Ever since my parents died, it's been a larger ambition of mine to have what I lost... a family in a rural community, just so I can relive it all over again, and being a doctor secures that for me."

"I suppose that sounds nice," Finn replied, "but I could never have that."

"Why not?"

"I already told you. It isn't worth it."

"You want to secure a future for children, but you don't want to have kids?"

"You don't understand."

"Then what's the contradictory explanation for this gap of logic?"

"It's not to do with the logic," Finn replied in a fierce tone. "It's about me! I'm never going to have a family, so drop it!"

Tristan flinched at Finn's response. He stopped walking with him while Finn continued.

"You know, the smartest man I know is someone who's specialized in it all. You might know him," Tristan remarked. "There's no reason you can't go out and explore the world and learn all that there is to learn – I'm glad you have enough sensibility to understand the importance of family, and I hope in time you come to reconsider your approach towards it, but at the same time we're young and have time to pursue our interests. Perhaps instead of wasting your time with this senseless crap, you should put in some effort into what you're really passionate about."

Finn turned around and looked at Tristan.

"My life has meaning because of this 'senseless crap,' more meaning than ever before. I have no reason or motivation to do anything else."

Finn then continued to walk forward. Tristan looked to him, sighed and then continued to walk, walking behind him as they continued onwards to reach the natural gas plant.

Act 4, Scene 3

Charlemagne shielded his face as if he was staring at the sun. The heat of the fire was felt from where he stood. Miklos returned from the water, clenching his side. He then sat down on the shore.

"Are you alright?" Charlemagne asked, kneeling down next to him.

"Yeah…" Miklos replied. "I'll be fine."

"Good," Charlemagne responded, standing up and looking around him.

The tall grass of the clearing were lit aflame, but the gorge they were in appeared to be safe despite the smoke. However, they were equipped with oxygen should they need it.

"The fire won't burn at the field for long…" Charlemagne said, stepping back. "When it clears, contact Igor to get you out of here."

"Where are you going?" Miklos questioned.

"I'm sorry…" Charlemagne simply replied. "I have to know for certain that this is not my fault."

Suddenly, Charlemagne ran off and climbed up the cliffside to enter the forest fire ahead of him, covering himself from the whip of flames at the trees to his side to sneak through a gap in the forest that provided him an entry.

"Charles!" Miklos shouted. "Charles!"

Charlemagne ignored him, shielding his face by keeping it down as he went through, jumping atop of log and hopping into the forest to come to the other side. The intense sensation of heat had doubled. Charlemagne's face began to instantly sweat and his face grew red as though he had sat in the sun for too long. He looked around himself at the trees burning at his side. He continued inwards, rushing through at a calm, but rushed pace as he followed the safest ground at his feet. The floor was lit like brimstone with spots of embers that glowed. The bushes at his side and fallen logs had been replaced with flames that reached almost two meters tall. The worse flames came from the taller shrubs and the least painful to bear were from the fir and pine whose trunks had adopted a layer of fire that burned eternally up along the trunks of the trees, stretching upwards, into the smoke. Charlemagne looked upwards for a brief moment.

The smoke in the forest was thicker and consisted of a mustard color and fortunately due to the afternoon light, it was possible to see around. The smoke was also lower than outside the forest near the scientist's camp. Charlemagne took his compass out from his pocket and looked at it before putting it away. He then kept his head down as he continued along the narrow path that led him to a clearing in the forest. He stopped there to wipe his face with a handkerchief. He then took a moment to look behind him and then forward. He had reached a dead-end.

The light helicopter flew overhead and passed him above. Charlemagne looked behind again as if he was looking for something, or someone, and then looked ahead to where he needed to go. He brought his gloved hands towards a log that had fallen over and quickly pushed it forward, backing up as it fell and providing a path deeper into the forest. He then coughed before bringing his feet atop of the burning log and hopping over into a narrow path between some bushes on fire. Charlemagne rushed through this path, keeping his arms together and reaching the other side to hear the crack and split of wood above. He looked up and then backed away, jumping into the narrow path he came from and covering his head as the burnt branches fell down and crashed behind.

Charlemagne coughed again and then came onto his back to see in front of him. He turned his neck to look behind with regret. He then stood up and walked towards the burning wreckage, jumping over and continuing onwards. Charlemagne stopped again as he met a wall of dense trees packed together at the feet of some shrubs that created a firewall behind a stone creek that prevented him from going ahead. He instead went to the right and took his canteen from his backpack and opened it to drink some water before looking around. Charlemagne put his canteen away and then looked behind himself to the trees that were burning on the other side.

At the sight of these trees, he took his hatchet out and walked over. He looked at the tree and then back towards the firewall, and then without warning, he swung at the tree, chipping at the burning wood and sending embers outwards and into the water. He took another swing and then heard an uneasy tear of the fibers of wood that warned him to get out of the way as the tree fell over and across the creek to smother the bushfire on the other end.

Charlemagne looked at the mess he had created and then over to the bush. The trunk of the tree was still aflame, but had provided him an entry through the firewall. Charlemagne removed his backpack in the water and took out a fire blanket, bringing it over to the trunk and casting it over to create a surface he could climb onto near the bushes. He then brought his backpack back around himself and started to climb onto the fallen log, balancing himself and then rushing forward into the fire and reaching the other side. There, the trunk broke with the step of his feet, causing him to fall over to the left and land on the ground by some burning bushes.

The flames singed his jacket and caught his backpack on fire. Charlemagne immediately disassociated himself from the backpack, leaving it behind and then rushing forward. He brought his gloved hands onto the trunk of a burning tree, instantly removing them from the trunk, but not before looking up and then quickly covering his head as embers fell beneath him. Charlemagne held on for a minute before relaxing from his crouched position to look around. He stepped forward to the right of the fallen log and began to hop from space to space until he reached a space of ground with streaks of fire spread around as well as tall fir trees spread apart.

Charlemagne brought his hands into his pocket to take out his compass but returned his hand from his pocket without it. He checked his other pocket and returned with nothing from that pocket as well. He then stood in the midst of the forest, looking around and realizing that he had found himself lost in hell as he looked hopelessly in either direction before looking upwards towards the smoke in hopes of spotting the sun. Charlemagne then clutched for his mouth as he let out a hacked cough, stepping down onto one knee.

The crack of wood caused Charlemagne to jerk his face to the right as a tree was about to tip over. Charlemagne coughed and then ran forward, jumping over and landing onto the ground. He then continued to cough, gasping for air as he looked upwards to the smoke and tops of the trees. His skin, although red, was also looking to become slightly pale. Charlemagne clutched for his radio, pulling it from his belt and then tapping a red button at the top. The radio let off a loud alarm-like noise.

"M-" Charlemagne attempted to say, coughing and dropping the radio to his side.

Charlemagne clutched for his stomach instead and then turned to his side before everything went dark.

• • •

Charlemagne awoke with a mask at his face. He opened his mouth, seeing the gloved hand at the oxygen mask and person on his knees at his side. Charlemagne closed his eyes and kept them closed as he took simple breaths.

"Take it easy, Charles," Miklos said in a calm, but muffled voice.

After a minute, Charlemagne moved his hand and brought it to the mask to hold. Miklos took the opportunity to drink some water from his canteen before taking the mask away from his face and turning the valve on the tank off. Miklos had a gas mask over his own face with a tube that went into the oxygen tank placed on his back.

Miklos took his hands and brought one to Charlemagne's hand and the other behind his neck. He helped him sit up and then offered him the oxygen mask again so that he could continue to recapture his breaths. Miklos stayed on one knee as Charlemagne breathed.

Charlemagne looked to him after staring at the ground for several minutes.

"I'm sorry," Charlemagne said, "I didn't mean to force you into this mess."

"I'm required to protect you, and whether that be from terrorists or nature, I will protect you," Miklos stated. "You have no need to apologize, except maybe to yourself because this was certainly stupid of you to do."

Charlemagne nodded and then looked around himself.

"This hellish landscape seems unreal," Charlemagne commented, "and yet it is all too real as if truly the flames of hell. The beautiful nature of God is being eaten away by this destructive force and there is nothing in our power to stop it."

"If we don't get out now, we'll be consumed too," Miklos warned. "Let me help you onto your feet."

Miklos took the oxygen mask from Charlemagne and cut off the source of oxygen to the mask so that he could help Charlemagne back onto his feet.

"What happened to your backpack?" Miklos questioned.

"Oh, it caught on fire," Charlemagne casually responded, "but never mind that – hand me your compass."

Miklos took his compass from his pocket and gave it to Charlemagne. Charlemagne examined the direction around them and pointed the compass into the right direction.

"Come on," Charlemagne said, walking forward.

The two walked through the forest together. Miklos took an axe at the side of his backpack and held it in his hand. They trekked uphill and then reached a tighter space with more bushes to navigate around. Miklos attempted to swing at the bushes as if the axe was a machete, but his attempts to clear the bush proved futile.

Instead, the two continued to walk through with careful steps, ducking every so often for falling debris before they reached another dead-end. The two ducked again at the sound of splitting wood, keeping their head down as a wind of hot air and embers rushed past them. The debris that had fallen blocked their exit from the dead-end they had arrived at. Charlemagne looked at the debris in shock and then around them in the circle they were trapped in.

"There's no escape," Miklos complained, checking all angles.

"We'll need to push through," Charlemagne suggested.

"Are you honestly mad?" Miklos reacted, looking to him.

"What other choice do we have but to stay here and die of dehydration?" Charlemagne replied. "The least we can do is find the space with the least likelihood to be dense – that way, we can risk setting ourselves on fire and being able to put ourselves out."

The two continued to look around.

"There," Miklos said, pointing forward. "At least a meter in length – see behind?"

Charlemagne looked at where Miklos had pointed at and saw that there was space behind it for them.

"I will go first," Miklos suggested, turning off the valve of his oxygen tank and removing it from himself. "I will let you know if it is good."

"No," Charlemagne denied. "I will go."

"With all due respect," Miklos interrupted.

"I know, it's your job," Charlemagne replied, looking back to the space with focused eyes.

"Please, stay here," Miklos said to him. "Allow me."

Charlemagne nodded and looked to Miklos as he looked to the space. He took a deep breath and then sprinted forward, covering his face as he jumped into the fire, catching himself aflame and causing him to scream out. Miklos disappeared behind the fire, causing Charlemagne to panic and run after him, removing his helmet and bringing the hood of his jacket over his head. He also covered his face and jumped into the flames, feeling his body burn instantly with the fire and cause a twitching pain. Charlemagne landed on the ground and attempted to put himself out by rolling. He then stood up as he shouted and looked forward to where he saw the cliffside that looked down upon a river.

"Charles!" Miklos yelled out from below.

Charlemagne instantly rushed forward and jumped overboard, into the water, dunking himself and then coming out. The waters of the stream were calm. Miklos swam to the shore and climbed out of the river to sit atop of a rock. He took deep breaths and laid back. Charlemagne swam towards him and landed on the beach. He looked outwards to the fire and the two took a moment to recover before looking at the river. He then relaxed again as his eyes went back and forth. Charlemagne looked to Miklos.

"We can use this river to get out," Charlemagne said, looking to Miklos. "We can follow the river – do you have a map? I need to see if this river flows into the fire or away from it."

Miklos removed his backpack, rummaged through and took out a map of the forest. He then handed it to Charlemagne who opened it and examined where they could be based on where the landing site was.

"I approximate we are here," Charlemagne suggested, pointing at a river on the map. "There are no other rivers for quite a distance, and I don't believe we've travelled very far. The river runs into the forest, into the oldest parts that have been set on fire for almost a week and gone out. If we follow the shallow parts of the river, swim where necessary, and keep our respiration to a minimum, we might have decent odds at getting out of this forest alive. Does your radio work?"

Miklos nodded as he switched channels from the mic at his chest. He then gave a light smile as he looked to Charlemagne.

"Perfect," Charlemagne remarked. "We can radio Igor to meet us wherever we arrive to."

"Your genius comforts me," Miklos simply remarked, "even if you have stupid ideas from time to time, you seem to figure a way out."

Charlemagne gave a shy smile. The two took another moment to relax before they returned to the water and proceeded to carry on with the river to guide them.

Act 4, Scene 4

Finn and Tristan climbed up the trail of a hill, reaching the top and looking forward towards the natural gas facility below. The sun faced them as it started to make its way towards the westward horizon. Each of the boys laid down on the grass on their stomachs. Finn produced some binoculars while Tristan looked with his own eyes to the large facility below.

The natural gas plant consisted of a mess of pipes, metal scaffolding and catwalks, and large cylindrical metal chimneys. In total there were approximately three chimneys each at the end of three wide towers with stairs and catwalks along the side. The towers were connected together by beams and additional supports as well as pipes. Each chimney had a circular catwalk approximately two meters before the very top with ladders along the sides from the tops of the towers. The towers only went as high as half of the chimney, which was at least ten to fifteen meters tall.

From where the boys had arrived from, there was a moat around the perimeter of the facility made of concrete, sloped and creating an artificial canal that was dried out and empty. The entire facility was surrounded by a chain link fence on the inner side of this canal with poles that had cameras facing either side, pointed downwards.

On the other side of the facility, there were portable offices to the left corner with a similar appearance to a motel with balconies at the front on the second level, above a porch on the ground level. At the right corner was a concrete structure, one-story in height and similar in appearance to a bunker. At the left-side of the 'bunker' was a downward ramp that went to the presumable entrance of the structure. The structure was next to an offshoot of the canal that went into the facility and through the fence. Beneath the fence was a concrete wall – the offshoot was connected to the other canal by an open pipe. On the opposite, left-side of the facility were some spherical tanks on struts. Several workers could be seen in reflective vests and orange jumpsuits with yellow hardhats milling around.

The entire compound, beyond the canal, surrounded plains, which in itself was surrounded by trees. There was a road on the other side of the facility, behind a parking lot that was enclosed in its own fence before reaching a checkpoint that connected to a road that was an offshoot to the main freeway. Beyond the freeway were some hills and the setting sun.

"So, what's the plan?" Tristan questioned.

"Trust me, I know what to do," Finn responded. "I've had an infiltration plan set for a week. First, we need to get inside, disguise ourselves…"

"… and find incriminating documents that state expansionist efforts," Tristan said. "How we're going to get through all this security before us is beyond me."

"You see those poles with the cameras pointed to the outer fence," Finn remarked, "those aren't cameras, but sensors that detect motion around the perimeter. Do you see those small rectangular packets on the fence? They're sensors that detect any tampering with the fence."

"You seem to know this place," Tristan replied.

"I did my research," Finn simply said, shrugging. "There are approximately three security guards in total – one doing alarm monitoring, and another two patrolling in the least. I see one at the west-side, but not the other."

"What if we get caught?" Tristan questioned.

"We won't get caught," Finn replied. "Trust the plan, Tristan. Everything is going to be alright. Now give me your warden jacket."

"What? Why?"

"Because you're too baby-faced to pose as a Defra warden," Finn remarked, "honestly, we've been out here for a week and you've not grown much in terms of facial hair. Not to mention they'll see right through your Canadian accent."

Tristan looked at Finn. He had shaven each morning, but had more of a stubble grown in the last hours than Tristan in the entire week. He took out the warden jacket from his pack and gave it to Finn. Finn turned around on the grass and proceeded to loosen his belt so that he could take off his flannel shirt. He ditched his baseball cap and removed his tank top underneath before putting on his flannel shirt again, buttoning up and tucking his shirt into his shorts before tightening his belt again. Tristan looked at him as he almost transformed in appearance.

"What about me?" Tristan questioned.

"Stay here," Finn cautioned. "Like I said, they'll pin you as a kid straight off the bat."

"I want to go in, especially to make sure that you look for documents instead of doing any sort of sabotage," Tristan argued. "It's non-negotiable. Either I come with you, or you don't go in at all."

Finn looked at him with an annoyed face.

"Fine, the baby-faced baby can come. I'll look for a disguise once we're in. Okay?"

Finn stood up from the grass and looked down. Finn put on his baseball cap again and looked to Tristan.

"Ready?" Finn questioned.

"Yeah."

"Let's go then," Finn replied, starting to move down the hill. "Stay close to me."

The two proceeded to head down the hill, reaching the edge of the canal. Finn climbed down and the two then slid down the side of the canal to reach the bottom where a puddle of water was all that was left.

Finn looked in both directions as Tristan caught up. He then led him down the right and around the corner to reach a concrete pipe poking out from the side and going into the natural gas plant. Finn climbed in and was forced to crouch as he went forward. Tristan followed from behind. The tunnel was short and led to a metal grate connected to the tube by a lock. Finn detached himself from his backpack and took out a hairpin as well as his knife. He then set off to pry the lock while Tristan kept his eyes on their behind.

"Got it," Finn proclaimed, detaching the lock and tossing it down.

Finn picked up the grate and moved it aside. He then rummaged through his backpack, returning the hairpin and knife before taking some other things.

"Leave your pack here," Finn ordered. "We'll return back here before we leave, okay?"

"Sure," Tristan replied, detaching himself from his pack.

Finn put something into the jacket, which Tristan looked suspiciously at. Tristan extended his hand to Finn's shoulder, forcing him to turn around.

"No explosives," Tristan warned.

"I know," Finn replied, brushing him off. "Come on – let's move on."

Finn continued forward and came to the other side of the pipe. He stretched out his legs and then stood up in the canal. At the end of the canal was a ladder leading upwards. Finn kept himself low and moved forward while Tristan lagged from behind and caught up to him towards the ladder.

"One of us goes up to take a peak," Finn warned.

Tristan nodded. Finn volunteered himself to go upwards the ladder and poke his head out and take a look. Tristan looked around, keeping watch of their surroundings before Finn rushed down, sliding down the ladder to the bottom of the canal. He then brought his back against the wall, motioning Tristan to do the same. Finn looked tense. Tristan could hear the voices of some people speaking in a Scottish accent above as well as the shuffle of feet. Finn looked away from Tristan and then towards him. The two looked at each other. The voices of the people above disappeared, leaving them alone.

"Too close," Finn remarked, "no way we can go up there without dressing you a worker."

"Oh, so now you need me?" Tristan replied. "I can't imagine what your plan would have been without me."

"I would have just dressed as a worker, idiot. Come on, let's see where this tube leads."

Finn broke off from the wall and went towards a concrete pipe that went below the bunker. Tristan followed and crouched down to follow Finn through the tube. There was a horrible stench in the pipe, one of rotten eggs, most likely methane.

The tunnel was longer than the one separating the compound from the outside, but there was a light at the end, which gave promise to an alternate plan. Finn looked out of the tunnel and pulled his legs out. He then hopped out, allowing Tristan to follow behind and see where they had come to. It was some sort of sewer system. Tristan rubbed his arms as he felt goose bumps develop. The room was chilled.

"Bad memories," Tristan muttered, examining the room.

The boys had come to a small room with a trench in the middle that ran across. The trench was low and at either side were platforms as well as a bridge in the middle connecting the two. There was a ladder to their left and various piping in the room. The room was similar to the boiler room aboard the RVS Ingstad as well as the Nattau County Water Treatment Plant, but darker with only light bulbs hanging from reinforced wires from the ceiling lighting the room. They were alone.

Finn climbed up the ladder and came to the top. He then walked forward as Tristan followed from behind and caught up

"I assumed this would have been the ideal time to strike," Finn remarked to Tristan in a quiet voice. "About the time people have set off home, and thus crazy enough to have a little mischief unseen."

"Not at night?" Tristan questioned.

"No, too quiet and people are too alert to any small out of place detail."

At the end of the room was a metal door. Finn brought his hands to the door and attempted to open it. The door knob was unlocked for them to exit and come to a basement corridor with incandescent lights and laminate floors. The ceiling was suspended and there was an absence of people around. Finn fiddled with the doorknob of the door they came through, checking the other side to see if it was locked or unlocked. It was locked, so Finn wedged the door bolt so that it wouldn't lock on them. He then stepped away from the door and looked around for a moment before seeing a room with plaque stating, 'Men's Locker Room.'

Finn went towards the room with Tristan behind. He entered and came to a changing room separated between a bathroom on the left set with showers, toilet stalls, urinals and sinks, and a space on the right with lockers around the perimeter and benches in the middle. In the small corridor they separated the two different rooms was a rack with jumpsuits next to a laundry basket.

"Here we go," Finn said, looking at the jumpsuits. "Nab one of them for yourself. Hurry before we're caught."

Tristan looked at the jumpsuits and then over to the showers. "Jeez, it would be really nice to have a decent shower before we left…"

Finn looked to him and then to the showers.

"Snap out of it," Finn cautioned, "and get dressed," he added, taking a jumpsuit and shoving it into Tristan's grip.

Finn took a reflective vest off of the coat rack as well as a hardhat helmet. Tristan took the jumpsuit and went over to the bench to get dressed. He removed his shorts and then his hiking shoes, pulling up the jumpsuit before putting on his shoes again.

"I'm sure that's fine," Tristan said, looking at his shoes. Tristan then went over and took a reflective vest and hardhat helmet.

Finn had found a clipboard and pen on the floor and looked to Tristan.

"Do us a favor and don't speak when we leave," Finn requested.

Finn then left. Tristan followed him. The two returned to the corridor where they saw some people coming down from a hall ahead. Finn walked towards them, avoiding eye contact and walking straight past them. Tristan followed him from behind. Once the two people had passed them and disappeared, Finn turned around to Tristan.

"Maybe you go ahead," Finn remarked. "You're supposed to be leading me, not the other way around."

"Right," Tristan replied. "Sorry."

The two changed positions and Tristan led Finn down the long corridor and towards the exit outside. Tristan pressed a handicap button to have the door open automatically. The two then walked outside and came to the end of the exit underground.

Tristan looked ahead to the offices and started to lead Finn towards them.

The boys crossed the front of the compound and came up the stairs to the porch in front of the offices. Tristan attempted to open the door inside, but the door was locked.

"Uh oh," Tristan muttered to himself.

"God," Finn cursed as Tristan turned around and came down the steps. "Take me to the other side – I'll jimmy my way in."

Tristan went around to the back of the portable where there were only windows. The two looked at the windows.

"Excuse me?" a man questioned in a lowland accent.

The two both turned towards the man. It was a security officer in a vibrant reflective jacket and black cargo pants.

"Can I help you?" the man then asked.

Tristan looked to Finn and then back to the security guard who was looking at him.

"Uh," Tristan stuttered in his authentic accent, "I mean," he said mimicking a stereotypical Scottish accent. "I'm looking for the chief engineer. Man here says he's from Defra and needs to talk with my supervisor, but I can't find 'im."

"Who are you?" the man asked.

"Cunningham," Finn stated. "Finn Louis Cunningham, and I need to speak with the current supervisor about an urgent matter."

Finn brought a hand into his jacket and took out a wallet. He then took out a driver's license and presented it to the man. The man looked at the license and then gave it back to Finn. Tristan looked at the license and the name it posed. The license had Finn's picture and the full name, 'Finn Louis Cunningham.'

"I need to speak with whoever is in charge of the site right now," Finn declared. "I'm working with Defra and the subject is over the wildfires that could pass through these lands."

"There aren't any trees in these parts," the man objected.

Finn looked at the security guard like he was an idiot.

"The fires can travel over grasslands as well and send winds of embers," Finn explained. "This entire site is at risk."

"Right then," the security guard responded, "follow me and I'll radio the site supervisor for you."

"Thank you," Finn replied, turning to Tristan "and thank you for helping me out. You can get back to work, I think."

"It's no problem," Tristan responded, watching them off.

Tristan then looked at the windows behind the portable and hesitated to act. He walked over to a back door, up some stairs onto a platform, and tried to open it. The door was locked. He looked into a window next to the door and saw that he could unlock it if he got through the glass. Tristan made a fist and shielded his fist with the sleeve of his jumpsuit. He then punched the glass and cringed in anticipation of an alarm.

No alarm went off. Tristan unlocked the window and then slid it open for him to climb through. He then entered an office space and looked. There were desks lined against the walls of the immediate office space around him, which went into a corridor with individual offices for more important personnel before coming to the reception office where the exit was. He started his search here, opening drawers to find useless papers, and conveniently seeing keys left atop of handles of filing cabinets for him to unlock.

Tristan avoided the offices in the middle as he came to the back room and searched around. He checked the drawers of each desk and filing cabinets before going to the manager offices in the middle, breaking the doors open through the glass windows in the middle of them, and opening them one by one.

Once Tristan was finished in the last office, he sighed and looked to the computer.

"What was I expecting," Tristan muttered, "if there's anything incriminating, it'll be in a digital file. I'm not Moira though…"

Tristan jumped as he heard a knock on the door. He looked out the window behind him to see that it was not Finn, causing him to duck down. The man knocked again. Tristan breathed steadily and waited for the man to leave. Once several minutes had passed, he peaked out and looked. The man was gone.

"I'm out of here," Tristan said to himself, leaving the office and going the way he came.

Tristan opened the rear door and exited down the steps, going away from the back of the office and bumping into another worker.

"Who are you?" the man questioned in a local accent. "I don't recognize you."

"I'm new," Tristan simply replied, looking pale.

"No you're not," the man stated.

"I am," Tristan insisted, attempting to walk past him, "I have to go."

Tristan walked a meter away from him before the man stopped him.

"Let go of me!" Tristan complained.

"Security!" the man shouted.

"What?" Tristan questioned, looking around.

Tristan caught sight of Finn nearby. He went over to them and intervened.

"Excuse me," Finn said to the worker, looking at both him and Tristan, "I think I smell a gas leak over there – this site is not safe!"

"What?" the man questioned.

"There they are!" the security guard from earlier said with another worker, an elderly man. "Stop right there! The two of you!"

Finn and Tristan both froze.

"The police have been contacted and are on the way!" the security guard shouted.

"Uh oh," Finn remarked, stepping back.

"What do we do?" Tristan questioned.

"You're not going anywhere," the worker in front of them said, grabbing them.

"Hands off, mate," Finn barked, slapping his hand away and grabbing it.

Finn took the man down to the ground, causing the security guard to rush towards them. Finn grabbed Tristan and brought him to the ground, shielding him. Tristan then heard an explosion. A terrible roar and shriek of metal. Tristan looked behind him and saw a large burst of flames pass over them, causing him to hide his face again.

Once the flame had dissipated, Finn got on one knee to look around. There were some additional explosions heard, but none that worried Finn as he looked to Tristan and helped him up.

"Come on!" Finn shouted to him. "We're leaving!"

Tristan didn't object and stood up. The two then ran towards the canal and climbed down one by one. Tristan went after Finn, bringing himself carefully around the edge and starting to gently climb each rut. A secondary larger explosion roared and a large combustion of flames flew overhead. Tristan shielded his face with his arm before jumping down. The two took cover until the flames settled. They then rushed towards the pipe where their packs were, equipping themselves before leaving the way they came, running and ditching their hardhats and vests in some bushes as they escaped from the blaze behind them.

Act 4, Scene 5

Charlemagne and Miklos continued down the river and eventually came out of the forest fire and entered a dark and miserable world instead. The trees at either side of them continued to burn, but were singed, black and skinny. The trees that were no longer burning were simple trunks with no branches, leaves or pine needles. The entire area around them was devoid of life. There was no grass nor bushes. The dirt at their feet was grey and mixed with ash. The skies above them were grey and the clouds of smoke were thick. In comparison to the forest behind, they were in no danger to the leftover fires that continued to burn. The area smelt of smoke.

The pair stopped at a river bank and came ashore. Charlemagne looked at the area around him with a somber face as though he was about to cry. The forest was calm and quiet. There was nothing to be heard or anything to hear. The two rested for a moment on the beach from their long hike along the river and enjoyed some morsel of dried meat. Once they were done, Miklos looked to Charlemagne.

"Should I contact Igor and have the helicopter come to us?" Miklos questioned.

"Not yet," Charlemagne responded. "I want to take a moment to walk around."

Charlemagne stood up from where he sat and stretched his back. He then turned around and looked out to the forest behind them. Miklos stood up and walked to stand next to him. They proceeded to walk into the ruins of the forest together.

The two quietly walked along without issue. Charlemagne looked at the trees and walked for about ten minutes before stopping to bring his hands to the burnt sides of a tree.

"You know," Charlemagne said, looking to Miklos, "ninety-percent of forest fires are caused by human hands. People are so quick to blame a widespread paranoia of so-called increased droughts, when it is our own who are at fault – a shift of blame notorious of the media whose people and people alike can never accept responsibility."

Charlemagne sighed and produced some binoculars from his jacket. He looked out and around the area. He spent several minutes before lowering the binoculars and shaking his head.

"I have seen a lot of travesty in my life, but none as widespread as this," Charlemagne remarked, stretching his arms out, "because this... this is depressing and fills me with sadness."

Charlemagne looked out around him. The barren and burnt forest went for miles around them with the smoke of the ongoing fire towards the southwest.

"The neglect of the forest that nourished us since the birth of our people is a great neglect," Charlemagne remarked. "A betrayal of man against his mother; mother nature. A betrayal of man against God who entrusted man to be a steward of the Earth and all of His creations from the smallest flower to the largest beasts. What a sad sight this is... the loss of wildlife, the loss of vegetation, and for what? If this forest fire were caused by accident, accidents are to be forgiven, but deliberate? I ache to know of the soul, or soulless fiend, who could orchestrate such a crime against humanity and disruption of the natural cycle of life. If this were naturally caused, it would simply be the way of life like natural death, but I refuse to believe that this was natural. There is no statistical chance that the climate of England could orchestrate something like this – it was simply not her time, which only leaves man to blame. What is to be done of man?"

Charlemagne sighed and continued to walk, bringing his hands behind his back as he continued his stroll through the forest with Miklos nearby.

"The trees that have survived are susceptible to disease, fungus, insects... their misery does not end with the fires," Charlemagne remarked, "and the animals that have survived have lost their homes, sources of food and nourishment – livelihood. The soil, mixed with ash, has become hydrophobic and with England's climate of endless rainfall, it will become the inevitable grounds of storm water runoff, taking debris and sentiment into the nearby streams, promoting pollution and other malaise."

Charlemagne continued to walk, looking upwards to the grey smoky skies.

"This smoke, toxic to breathe in as I have experienced, will haunt those with asthma and other respiratory diseases, and to some, produce some sort of respiratory disease that will make it difficult to breath."

Charlemagne sighed again. He stopped as they approached a clearing of debris. He took a deep breath and turned around to face Miklos.

"Even if I do find some sort of evidence that could suggest that Cabernet Industries was not behind the forest fire, who would believe me? Who would I convince?" Charlemagne questioned. "Simply being here depresses me. Call Igor and have the helicopter come for us. It's time we returned back to the warden station – I've wasted time and put both our lives in danger for nothing. If there will be an investigation, the authorities can carry it out."

"Yes, Charles," Miklos replied, taking the microphone connected to his radio at his jacket. "Charlie-One to Charlie-Six. We are ready for evac – do you have my coordinates?"

Miklos and Charlemagne waited for a response.

"Copy," Igor responded over the radio. "We have your location. ETA ten minutes."

"Copy that," Miklos replied.

Charlemagne looked to Miklos and nodded to him. He then turned around and looked back out to the forest, walking over to a turned over log and sitting down to observe the aftermath of the fire as he waited. Charlemagne focused on the damage for a minute and then closed his eyes. He kept them closed and took steady, deep breaths.

In less than ten minutes, the two of them could hear the sound of the helicopter rotors approaching them from the east. Charlemagne opened his eyes and looked forward to the light helicopter. He stood up and looked to Miklos who stood up from where he was resting on one knee. Miklos took a canister from his belt and unclipped it. He then tossed it into the clearing, producing a purple smoke for the helicopter to see.

"You know what, Miklos," Charlemagne remarked, "even with all this destruction, it is true that they say that nothing is of absolute evil, as there is some good to be seen here. Life will prevail, always and forever, and a new forest will thrive in the wreckage. Disease and invading species have been eradicated in the least, and the forest can be given care and attention to grow anew. I will have to contact Allodia and see what can be done... even if man is to blame for the fire, man is also able to do good and should never be impeached because he too is a part of nature and his actions should be accounted into the natural cycle even if they are devastating and grandiose, random and sporadic. Only God should be seen as external to nature – He is the Creator of nature. Who is comparable to the glory of God? None. Not man – never man. One must never forget that man too is a part of nature – man who makes mistakes," he said, looking at the palm of his hands, "but is given the opportunity to repent due to the almighty mercy of God..."

Charlemagne looked to Miklos. He appeared to be exhausted and tired. Charlemagne smiled to him.

"How long has it been, Miklos?" Charlemagne asked, thinking for a moment before looking back at him. "You were only seventeen when we met – you lied to me that you were older, but I had empathy for you and your background – abandoned when you were young, a child soldier."

Miklos looked to Charlemagne.

"Even before when I had met Tristan, I already had a son," Charlemagne stated, "even before I conceived one with Manon at that matter. You, Miklos. I am a fortunate man, even if I am not a good man at that – all of my fortunes, I do not deserve, or am I being modest?"

Miklos nodded and then looked to Charlemagne. He let out a sigh.

"You took me in when no one else would," Miklos remarked. "I admired you – I am honored that you consider me in such a light, because I considered you like my father, even if I had attempted to kill you in Egypt... I don't think I would have ever have been able to forgive myself if something had happened to you, no less because of my own hands."

"You're forty-five years old, Miklos," Charlemagne stated. "It's time I stop placing you in such danger – it's time to retire from the field. I can move you to a safer position in Harlech if you'd like."

"Please, Charles," Miklos said, shaking his head, "I am not as old as you yet, and yet you continue to join us as if you were still as youthful as you were when we first met. I will retire when it is my time to."

Charlemagne nodded. He let out a sigh.

"We have to go and look for Tristan – I can't waste any more time with this side quest of mine," Charlemagne remarked. "He thinks he's with my biological son and is out there alone with this lad. I have to look for him and make sure he is okay..."

The light helicopter arrived towards the pair, hovering downwards and landing in front of them. Charlemagne went over as Igor approached them.

"Mr. Cabernet," Igor said, "what happened?"

"I got a little sidetracked, but we're fine," Charlemagne replied. "Just take us back to the ranger station, Igor. I've had enough of this forest fire -- I need to go look for my sons!"

"Of course, Mr. Cabernet," Igor replied, helping Charlemagne onto the helicopter.

Miklos sat down at the bench to the side of the helicopter. Once they were secured, the light helicopter flew upwards and off, away from the ruins of the forest and south towards Otterburn.

Act 5, Scene 1

The light helicopter returned to the warden station at the Otterburn Entrance to the national park, setting down at the helipad as the sun set for the day. The crew left the helicopter and walked back towards the warden station, entering the manor and going into the private area in the back. Charlemagne took Miklos and Igor to the war room where the head warden was with several other wardens.

In comparison to earlier in the day, the room had settled even if it was still busy with wardens taking phone calls. The head warden was with his female companion and updating the map with a marker to outline the extent of the fire in Tarset Forest. Since they had left in the afternoon, the fire had expanded almost a kilometer to the current fire line.

"With all the media attention and intensity of the situation, I'm surprised the Secretary of Defra isn't here with you all," Charlemagne stated. "How goes it?"

The head warden looked at him and didn't instantly reply. He finished making a mark on the map before looking to Charlemagne.

"No, she's too busy at her retreat in Fiji, I'm afraid," the head warden jibed. "Come to think of it, I think most of us will be needing a vacation after this fire is dealt with."

The warden closed the marker he was using and then thanked his female partner.

"Thank you for returning the scientists unharmed," the head warden finally said. "I had an earful from them about their equipment, but at least they were saved from the fires."

Charlemagne nodded.

"Is there anything else that you need from us?" Charlemagne questioned.

"Thankfully, not at this moment," the head warden responded, looking at Charlemagne. "We will let you know tomorrow if anything comes along, but for now, rest."

"I wish I could, but there is a matter I need to discuss with you," Charlemagne said, taking a deep breath.

Charlemagne explained to the head warden how Tristan had gone missing, avoiding the details of the river, but keeping to the fact that he had a team of three mercenaries in search of him. He then asked for permission to search the forest for him before the fires caught up to him. The head warden nodded.

"Of course," the head warden stated, "if there is anything you need from us, please do not hesitate to ask. Please, keep me updated on the situation of your son."

"Thank you," Charlemagne replied, nodding to him.

Once Charlemagne had finished speaking, he left with Miklos and Igor.

Charlemagne looked to Miklos as they walked back into the corridor of the station. Charlemagne took a deep breath.

"It's helped that we've cultivated a relationship with that chap," Charlemagne said to Miklos. "Tristan is now our top priority."

"Yes, Charles," Miklos replied.

The three of them returned to the public space of the station. He came to the lounge and saw Diana there with Hardrada and Holger as well as the scientists he had rescued. They were watching television, which was currently running adverts.

The scientists looked to Charlemagne as he entered the room. Charlemagne looked to them. The group had been arguing.

"Hello," Charlemagne greeted.

"Are you going to pay for our lost equipment, Mr. Cabernet?" the man with the circular sunglasses asked.

"Perhaps I'm willing to make a generous donation," Charlemagne replied, "depending on the subject of your studies and the importance of them to the general knowledge."

"We were studying the fire," the man responded, "it's cause and its effects"

"Oh yeah, and what had you found?" Charlemagne then asked. "Man-made or climate change?"

"Not climate change," the man replied, "for sure. Climate change is not a definitive conclusion to any wildfire because there simply isn't enough information to attest to it. The real question is whether a wildfire is natural or human caused, and the evidence suggests human caused."

"Lightning is the most common cause of a natural wildfire, but the weather patterns for the region have not been hot or dry enough," the woman with blonde hair next to him stated, "and there hasn't been any storms in the area, so that leaves dry lightning, but like I said, it hasn't been hot enough for it all to spiral out of control as it has."

"The area the fire started is a conservation area – no campers are allowed to cross those parts," the man also stated, "which only leaves malice."

"Breaking news," the TV reported, "explosion at Cunningham Natural Gas Plant in Roxburghshire has been confirmed to be the product of domestic terrorism. The BBC has received images of what are believed to be two suspects involved in this evenings bombing at the power station."

Charlemagne looked at the TV as it projected images of the gas plant and the aftermath of an explosion that had hit the plant.

"Oh, here we go again with this," the man complained, rolling his eyes, "there's your culprit – Aidan Cunningham and his billion dollar petroleum empire…."

"Turn that off," the woman requested, taking the remote control from the man.

Diana's eyes widened as she saw the grainy photo on the television screen.

"Wait!" Charlemagne shouted.

The scientists looked at him as he looked at the screen and photo. The photo was taken from closed-circuit television (CCTV) security cameras at the natural gas plant and displayed two figures, both wearing reflective vests and hardhats, and one in a jumpsuit and the other in a blue jacket with shorts. The image was taken from an angle at a doorway. The boy in the jumpsuit was noticeably identifiable as Tristan, while the boy in shorts was less identifiable, but Charlemagne looked at him with more focus while Diana looked at Tristan.

The image did not stay on the screen for long as it returned to the view of the news anchor. The image was minimized and placed at the corner of the screen.

"A manhunt is underway in the county to locate the duo who had disappeared shortly after the blasts… emergency crews have been on scene, called prior to the explosions due to two suspicious individuals roaming about, and various injuries have been reported. Anybody with information of the two suspected assailants have been directed to contact Metropolitan Police, Special Branch. In other news…"

Charlemagne looked towards Diana as soon as the image disappeared. He then looked to Miklos.

"Right… Miklos, I need to speak with you and your men, in private in the other room, please," Charlemagne said, leaving the lounge and going across to the education hub.

Miklos, Igor, Hardrada and Holger followed and came to the other room. Diana followed them, but didn't enter the room.

Holger closed the door behind them and Diana stuck near the door to listen by keeping her ear to the door.

"Igor, see if you can find a copy of that image of Tristan and that other lad on the internet," Charlemagne ordered. "Miklos, get into contact with Lukas for an update onto their efforts. We need to find these two before the authorities do…"

"Yes, Charles," Miklos replied, taking out his satellite phone. "I'll phone Lukas right now and brief him about the current situation."

"Thank you, and once you're done, I need you to get into contact with Mr. Heavner… I need every detail from that… special investigation brought to me for review."

Miklos left the room. Diana backed out of the way as Miklos exited and walked outside to make the phone call. The door was left open. Diana peaked in.

"Is there any possible efficient means to locate Tristan?" Charlemagne asked Igor.

"No," Igor replied, on his heavy-duty laptop. "We already assessed our options at the last search operation. All we can do is manually track him in the forest."

"He doesn't have his cellphone, so tracking his location via the SIM card is out of the option," Charlemagne cursed. "Damn! Someone get me a map of the county…"

Igor produced a copy of the map and gave it to Charlemagne. Charlemagne took the map and stretched it out on a table. He removed his jacket and rolled up his sleeves.

"I need my things… wait here until I return," Charlemagne said, leaving the room with his jacket.

Charlemagne walked towards the exit. Diana moved out of the way as Charlemagne left. He turned to her as he entered the foyer and gave an apologetic look on his face. He then went to her.

"Why don't you get some rest, Diana? We're going to do all we can to find Tristan before the authorities do," Charlemagne said.

"Who is that boy with him?" Diana questioned. "Why is Tristan with him? Why is he being blamed for a terrorist bombing? You said he was safe with Lukas."

Charlemagne looked at her with guilt.

"I'm attempting to find out and will tell you as soon as I can," Charlemagne assured her. "I don't want you to worry though."

"I'm worrying whether you like it or not, Tristan is family," Diana stubbornly said. "I'd be as invested in finding him as I would with you."

Charlemagne looked to her and sighed. He then left and went into the private space to go upstairs and pick up his laptop, his cellphone, some stationery, and then return downstairs. Charlemagne laid out his laptop on a table and then looked up as Miklos returned to the room.

"I've contacted Lukas – he says that Tristan's nearest tracks was at a camp near a farm," Miklos remarked. "I've also contacted Mr. Heavner and he'll be emailing you the details of that investigation…"

"Thank you," Charlemagne replied, typing into his laptop. "Take Holger and Hardrada with you and form an additional search team. Find him, Miklos, please… before the authorities do."

"Yes, Charles," Miklos replied, nodding.

Miklos then looked to the two Nords. They left the room and went outside. Charlemagne made some marks on the map to denote the location of the Cunningham Natural Gas Plant. Igor was at a nearby table.

"Igor, you'll be running intelligence and coordination between the teams," Charlemagne stated. "I want coordinates from Lukas and Miklos as they come in. Understood?"

"Yes, Mr. Cabernet," Igor replied.

"We're going to find Tristan…" Charlemagne said under his breath, "even if this takes all night."

Act 5, Scene 2

Finn and Tristan ran for almost a mile until they returned to an entrance at the forest, running through for almost another mile non-stop. Tristan had lowered the jumpsuit so that half of it was pulled down and the rest tied around him. He didn't have time to change out of the clothes, while Finn had abandoned the reflective vest and jacket, and rolled up the sleeves of his flannel shirt, untucked it, and detached the top buttons.

The duo reached a river in the Wauchope Forest where they stopped, panting and taking a moment to rest. The two breathed heavily while Tristan went to the water to wash his face. His hands were shaking. He continued to pant before looking to Finn who was smiling, looking the other direction.

"You idiot!" Tristan shouted at him. "Why did you do that?! I told you we wouldn't be violent, and you lied to me! Who knows how many people died because of that explosion!"

"Relax, I planted it in a good spot. Trust me," Finn responded. "I didn't promise you anything, anyways."

"Trust you? How can I trust you after what happened?!" Tristan questioned him. "Forget it, Finn. We're done!"

"Lighten up," Finn said to him, removing his backpack and sitting down. "Admit it – what we did today, was probably the most exhilarating thing you had ever done in your entire life."

"No," Tristan responded, "it was the most terrifying experience of my entire life. Do you not have any shred of remorse?"

"I'm sure they're all fine," Finn remarked, smiling again as he rummaged through his backpack. "Come on, take it easy. Had I not detonated the explosives, we would have had a run in with the cops and be in custody right now."

"In custody for a bit of trespassing and impersonation would have been fine," Tristan said with a grimace face. "I'm sure we might have also been pardoned given who owns that plant."

Finn took out a radio from his backpack and pulled out an antennae. He then switched the radio on, causing some country music to play before he started to change the channel.

"Authorities are in search of two young males associated with the bombing of a natural gas plant in Roxburghshire," the radio broadcasted. "The two males were seen via security cameras but have not been positively identified as of yet. In addition, police had received word prior to the explosion that two suspicious males had been loitering around the site, posing as a civil worker with the Department of Environment, Farmland, and Rural Affairs and the other as a technician."

Tristan looked away from Finn and back to the water.

"Aidan Cunningham, CEO of Cunningham Industries has yet to comment on the incident, but first responders are currently on scene and assisting in putting out the fire. No deaths have been reported, but multiple workers have been injured in the blast that has left the entire site devastated and the surrounding area without power. We will have more after this break…"

Finn turned off the radio.

"Cunningham Industries…" Tristan muttered. "No…"

Tristan turned around and looked at Finn.

"Cunningham," Tristan simply said to him. "Why did they say Cunningham?"

"Because that was Cunningham Natural Gas Plant," Finn explained.

Tristan grew pale.

"No, that doesn't make sense," Tristan replied. "I thought we were at a site owned by Cabernet Industries… isn't that your last name? Cabernet? Your father, the rich businessman you hate, isn't that Charlemagne de la Cabernet?"

"Who?" Finn questioned. "My biological father, regrettably, is Aidan Cunningham. I'm the son of the owner of Cunningham Industries. How else do you think I'd know that they were responsible for the forest fire?"

"I- I thought your father... but..." Tristan looked at Finn.

Tristan focused his eyes on Finn's appearance. He shook his head.

"Are you okay?" Finn questioned. "Seems like the adrenaline's got to you."

"I don't believe it," Tristan simply stated, "all this time... but you said that the father that raised you wasn't your actual father..."

Finn sighed and looked to Tristan, saying, "I was being dramatic... I wish he wasn't my dad, but the truth is that I'm the heir to the Cunningham throne, and if I'd have to guess, my father will attempt to cover up the incident to prevent any backlash against the family name. He'll know it was me... How else did you think that security guard eased up when I told him my name? He knew that I was the owner's son by my last name..."

"What if that security guard tells the police your name?" Tristan asked.

Finn shrugged.

"I don't care," Finn replied. "It'll destroy my father, which will work to my advantage."

"You're not a bit mature, are you?" Tristan remarked. "You don't care about yourself. You don't care about your future. All you care about is a bit of revenge against a man that didn't love you enough – that's all this is. I thought there was more to it – I stuck around because I thought you were someone else, but I was wrong. I don't even know who you are anymore."

Finn looked at him.

"What are you going to do? Leave? The authorities are looking for the both of us, and if you leave me, they'll be sure to find you, arrest you, and then you'll go to prison," Finn explained. "You're stuck with me now, whether you like it or not..."

"I don't like it..." Tristan said, shaking his head at him. "I don't like you. I don't like any of this. All I want to do is go home now."

"Shut up," Finn replied, standing up and grabbing his backpack.

Finn walked over to Tristan.

"Forget your life, Tristan," Finn stated. "You can't return to it – I can't return to my life, whether my father buries this or it comes to light. We're outlaws. Tristan, I like you, even if you are annoying and don't see eye to eye with me yet. Come with me and I can set you down the right path... just as it was fated. I've been thinking of a person like you all my life... someone who understands me and would be there with me all through out, and now you're finally here. Please don't leave me. I want you to come down the same path with me, just you and me, and we can live sheltered and fighting for a better life for the future of the white race. Please, join me."

Tristan looked at him awkwardly. Finn stepped away from him and looked out.

"I know a colony of people like us who live up north in Scotland," Finn said. "We can live there and start new lives – a new beginning for just the two of us."

Finn turned around again and looked to Tristan with a sympathetic face.

"I've never had a friend like you before, Tristan," Finn stated. "I've never really had a friend ever... Please don't leave."

Tristan looked at Finn. He looked closely at him, looking at his eyes and hair, his chin and cheeks, and his jaw and the scar under his left eye. His attention broke as he looked upwards in reaction to the sound of a helicopter passing overhead. The evening skies were orange.

"We should go," Tristan simply responded, "before those authorities find us less than a mile from the incident."

Tristan changed out of the jumpsuit and into his last pair of shorts. Once he was ready, the two set off again into the forest, walking instead of running, and walking until the sun finally set an hour or two later.

By that time, the two had established another camp set with a fire. They ate a dinner consisting of some salt-cured, smoked venison left over from their kill earlier today.

"You know," Finn remarked, "we could do some berry gathering – I've been putting it off, while we hike, but I have a book that can help us identify berries and test them if we're unsure. It'll add a little interest to our dinners and give us some needed vitamins. I'm worried about scurvy right now with our lack of vitamin C."

"Why don't we just bite the poisonous berry at the same time, while we're at it?" Tristan remarked in a hostile tone. "I don't want to do anything with you anymore – I don't even want to talk to you."

Finn frowned and lowered his head to look at his dinner. He set his dinner to the side and brought his arms around his legs as he raised his knees up. Tristan looked at him as he noticed Finn looking at him.

Finn sighed and stood up. He took some things from this backpack, including the bow and a pack of arrows, and proceeded to leave. Tristan watched him. Finn turned around to look back at him.

"I'm going to stay out for a bit," Finn stated. "Tent's set, so don't worry about me. I'll sleep under the stars for the night."

Finn then walked off and into the darkness. Tristan sighed and set his plate down. He maintained a frown.

"I'm an idiot," Tristan scolded, shaking his head. "Charles is going to kill me."

Neither of the boys finished their dinner, leaving half-eaten portions of their suppers. Tristan took the bucket and went to the river, fetching some water, and then going back to the fire only to return to see some rats scavenging around their dinner.

"Hey!" Tristan complained, rushing to the rats and shooing them off.

The rats were not too afraid of Tristan. He looked around for something to swat them with, picking up a large stick that he had collected as part of the kindling, and using it to poke the rat away. The rat finally left, running into the forest with the rest of Tristan's dinner.

Tristan sighed. He dumped the water atop of the grill, and then took the two plates, going over into the darkness of the wood to dump the leftover food in their latrine hole. He then returned to the camp and went to the water to wash the plates before returning to put away some tools that were lying around the camp, including the flint and steel, the plates and stationary, and other tools. Once he was done, the water had boiled for him to fill their water bottle. He then returned to the river to fetch some more water, setting the bucket near the fire as he prepared the tent with the blankets. He looked at what was available and decided to remove the sleeping bag, moving it outside across from the tent. He then returned and re-arranged the blankets for himself.

Once his bed was ready, Tristan took the pale of water and dumped it upon the fire, plunging himself into darkness. Tristan then sat down in front of the tent and looked ahead. He could see a bit of light not too far from the camp, possibly only a hundred meters away. Tristan could also hear the sound of a voice talking. He stood up, rummaged through Finn's backpack for a flashlight, and moved around the fire towards the forest. He entered and started to go through with careful steps until he could see that the light was produced by a lantern and the voice was the voice of a newscaster.

Tristan continued forward and hid behind a bush. He saw Finn on the ground ahead with the bow to his side, on the floor next to the bag of arrows. The radio and lantern were atop of a turned over log and Finn was on the ground with his feet in front of him, knees up, but apart. He was playing with his knife, spinning it and catching it in his hand with skill. Tristan got down on a knee as he observed him. He listened to the radio and to the voice of the man speaking in a posh Londoner accent.

"… the problem with these eco-activists," the man stated, "is that they don't think of the consequences of their actions. I'm not one to hold a grudge or target anyone, but if there has been any group that has targeted me more, it would be these eco-freaks who most likely blame my company for the unfortunate firestorm that's occurred in Berwick-Northumbria this week – and the problem stems beyond these extremists, but also to the Green Party and their lobbyists who constantly harass me."

"Is your company responsible for the fire at Berwick-Northumbria?" a man asked, presumably the radio broadcaster.

"No," Mr. Cunningham answered, "I am a man of the environment, my dear friend. I have been a strong advocate for the eco-friendly solutions to the energy crisis and the transition towards renewable resources. I have put in donations to the

Labor Party who make these promises – not these deep ecologists and Marxists in the Green Party. I am a believer in a green future, but despite all my actions and words, I am lined up as a sinister fellow. I am running out of patience with these people… and it hurts me. I would never, ever do anything that would hurt the poor forests of Britain. Why would I?"

"What about the recent meeting between your company and the Secretary of Defra? If you remember, an anonymous user online leaked a rumor on the notorious right-wing chat room known as 4Chan that there would be a large travesty in Berwick-Northumbria, an entire month before the fire had occurred, which coincided with a secret meeting between yourself and Ms. Gillian Thompson at your home in the Scottish Highlands. Photos were published with you and the Right Honorable…"

"Ms. Thompson is an old friend of the Cunningham family – our ties go back to the Second World War where my own father and hers served in the Royal Navy in the defeat of the fascist menace," Cunningham stated. "If you want my opinion on what these far-right extremists need to have happened to them, they ought to all be exterminated as we once handled them, in a tidal wave of fire and sulfur. They are the ones that should have to suffer through the flames of social media, and not myself and others accused. Hell, for all we know, these conspiracy theorists were the ones behind the fire – a self-fulfilled prophecy as it may. It's the only explanation, because my hands and by extension, my company, is free from any sort of arsonist activities."

"What of your son, who has been confirmed by police to be one of the two culprits in today's attack? Last year, he was arrested at one of your lumber sites for disturbing the peace at an eco-protest, so it is known to us that he is not fond of your company or its activities" the newscaster questioned. "Do you denounce him for his part?"

"All I can say is that I have no son," Mr. Cunningham replied. "No son of mine would go behind me back to sabotage the legacy of generations of Cunningham business. If this is how he feels of us, I only pray for his soul because he is has the spirit of a deluded and spiteful demon."

"Thank you, Mr. Cunningham, and thank you for taking the time to speak with us on our show," the newscaster replied.

"If I may, my dear friend, I have one more thing to say. In light of the recent fire, the slander against my family name, and now this case of domestic terrorism at my property, I would like to announce that I'll be having a press conference at my family lodge at Kielder Lake in Northumberland three days from now on the 20th, which will include an announcement into my company's response to both the rise of far-right extremism in Britain as well as this recent wildfire. Thank you."

"Thank you, Mr. Cunningham. We'll be back after these messages…."

Finn threw his knife towards the tree in front of him, piercing the bark and causing the knife to stick out. He stood up and went to the radio, changing the channel. The radio went to static. Finn then decided to turn it off completely before going over to the longbow and picking it up. He took a bag of arrows and brought it to the belt of his shorts. Finn went to the tree and took out his knife, returning it to its pouch, and then going all the way back in the clearing he had found and starting to shoot arrows.

Tristan watched him for a moment before backing up and going back to the camp with his flashlight guiding him. He turned off the flashlight and kept it with him as he went into the tent, bringing blankets over him and turning to his side to sleep. He kept his eyes open and took a deep sigh. He stayed like this for several minutes until finally closing them and drifting into sleep from the long day he had.

Act 5, Scene 3

Charlemagne sat in the learning hub of the ranger station past sunset with his reading glasses on, looking at the map at the table and his laptop, which included a report sent to him by Henry Heavner. He had made a slight progress in marking the map with Tristan's whereabouts, but had no definitive location. Igor had moved to a desk but had stepped out for a moment. Charlemagne took over for him with his radio placed on the desk. A lamp had been turned on in the corner of the room and the lampshade removed to provide some brighter light. The room was still moderately dimmed, but lit, nonetheless. Charlemagne traced his fingers from where he had lost Tristan in Leithope Forest to where he was last seen in Wauchope Forest.

Igor returned and sat down at his desk. He placed his headset back on.

"No updates," Charlemagne said, looking back at the map. "I'm going to take another hour and then retire for the night. You're free to retire for the night whenever you feel like it."

"Charlie-Six this is Charlie-One," Miklos broadcasted over the radio.

Charlemagne took his radio in hand and looked to Miklos.

"Go ahead, Charlie-One," Igor replied.

"Charlie-Six," Miklos said, "notify Charlie Actual that I've located the target at my coordinates: Thirty-Uniform, Whisky Golf, Two-Six-Seven-Zero-One, Three-Three-Four-Seven-Two."

Charlemagne gave Igor a thumbs up as he jotted down the coordinates and proceeded to look around on the map for them.

"Copy that, Charlie-One. Imperium copies," Igor responded.

"How shall I proceed?" Miklos replied.

"Stand-by," Igor said to him, looking to Charlemagne. "What do you want us to do?"

Charlemagne marked an 'X' where Tristan was. He then turned to Igor.

"Have Miklos send the helicopter to the other team, pick them up, and return here to escort me to Tristan," Charlemagne stated. "I want to be there in case he's non-compliant."

"Understood," Igor replied. "Charlie-One, Charlie Actual wants Team One to return to base to escort Imperium to the alpha target at once. Further orders upon his arrival. Charlie-Six out."

Igor removed his headset from his ears and looked to Charlemagne. Charlemagne held a smile on his face.

"Thank you for your help," Charlemagne remarked. "Get some rest – I'll take it from here."

"Thank you, Mr. Cabernet," Igor replied, taking his laptop and leaving the room.

Charlemagne looked at Tristan's coordinates on the map again and then sat down. Within fifteen minutes, the helicopter arrived and set down. Charlemagne put on his jacket and exited the warden station to go to the helicopter.

Lukas greeted him and walked over to the helicopter with him. Both him and his men seemed to be exhausted.

"What is your plan, Mr. Cabernet?" Lukas questioned, shaking his hand and then walking with him to the copter.

"I'm going to speak with Tristan, and if necessary, force him back – the situation has become dire and I won't have any of my sons imprisoned," Charlemagne stated. "Come on now, we have to fetch him before he escapes."

Charlemagne boarded the helicopter and the light helicopter lifted off. The night was quiet and there wasn't a cloud in sight as per usual. The stars were visible and the sky had a dark navy blue color to it. The night was bright. The helicopter proceeded west towards Wauchope Forest in Scotland and as they got closer, Charlemagne pointed to the forest.

"Land a kilometer from the location – we'll hike the rest of the distance to avoid startling them," Charlemagne said to the pilot.

"Yes, Mr. Cabernet," the pilot replied.

The helicopter flew towards the forest and lowered down in a clearing.

"I need to refuel," the pilot said to Charlemagne. "Contact me when you are ready."

"Will do," Charlemagne responded, exiting the helicopter.

Lukas, Brandan, and Lacplesis exited from the helicopter and proceeded to escort Charlemagne through the forest so that they could rendezvous with Miklos a kilometer away. Lukas led the way with a flashlight. The ambience of the forest at night consisted of crickets singing and owls hooting from time to time as well as the typical rush of water from streams as they passed by them. The air was cool, neither cold nor warm.

"Charlie-One to Charlie-Two," the radio went off with Miklos on the other end.

"Go ahead," Lukas replied in a quiet voice.

"What's your ETA?"

"Five minutes," Lukas responded.

"Copy," Miklos said, "we will meet you at a stream nearby to escort Imperium to the targets."

"Copy that."

The escort continued on as they had walked for almost twelve minutes in total before arriving at a stream. The team stopped and looked at either direction as they stood in the shallow waters. Charlemagne looked and saw Miklos appear from the bushes with his team.

"Thank you," Miklos said to Lukas before looking to Charlemagne. "We have Tristan and the other boy little more than a hundred meters from here in a camp they've made. How shall we proceed?"

"With ease," Charlemagne replied, "keep your men back and I'll go and speak with Tristan, have him brought out so we don't disturb the other boy, and attempt to make an appeal to his reason as well as find out what's happening. If he complies with us, we fly out with the two of them, and if either of them resist... sorry, if Tristan resists, we force him home, if the other boy resists, I don't suppose there'll be much we can do without kidnapping him, and that's not something I'm going to ask from you."

"Yes," Miklos responded, looking into the forest. "Let us go then and let me show you where they are."

"Thank you," Charlemagne replied, walking with him into the forest.

The entire squad, minus Igor, ventured into the forest and through. They walked for almost two minutes, and once they were near, Lukas and Miklos turned off their flashlights. Miklos showed Charlemagne what he had found as the two crouched. Charlemagne looked at the makeshift camp that had been made. The brightness of the moon allowed them to partially see without the need of a flashlight.

From where they had inserted, Charlemagne could see a boy in a sleeping bag in front of them, and across from a ditch in the ground, a tent with Tristan inside, sleeping with his head pointed out. The flaps of the tent were left open.

"Seems quaint," Charlemagne remarked in a whisper. "Hand me your flashlight..." he requested from Miklos.

Miklos handed him his flashlight. Charlemagne turned it on and then concentrated the light so that he got a straight beam. He then turned the light over to the camp and pointed it towards Tristan. Miklos looked at Lukas as Charlemagne focused the light on Tristan's eyes. He kept the light like this for almost two minutes before noticing Tristan starting to move around.

Tristan thrashed around and opened his eyes. He then covered them with his face before looking out and towards the bushes as he saw a bright light. Tristan rose up from the tent and shielded his eyes. Charlemagne widened the beam and brought the flashlight to his face. He then waved over to Tristan.

Charlemagne motioned Tristan to come over to him. Tristan looked at him with surprise and then over to Finn. He removed his blankets from himself and then crawled out of the tent to go towards the bushes, stopping as he snapped on a branch. Finn moved around in his sleeping bag but was not woken up. Tristan continued towards the Protection Squad and then got into the bushes.

Miklos put a hand over Tristan and the team began to lead him away from the camp until they were almost at the river. They then stopped there, Miklos and Lukas turned on their flashlights to give some light. Charlemagne looked to Tristan, opening his arms and hugging him.

"Oh, I'm so relieved that you're alive, my boy," Charlemagne said before parting from him. "What on Earth is wrong with you? You have a lot to explain to me about this terror nonsense."

"I *can* explain," Tristan replied. "After we separated, I landed on a beach and near a camp. There, I met this boy who was dressed as a boy scout. He was nice. He fed me. He told me he knew the forest and that he would take me to a ranger station so that I could reunite with you, but then I continued talking to him… He told me that his father was a rich businessman – a billionaire, and that he also hated his father. I was suspicious about that, and the more I looked at him, the more I was beginning to see you in him – your face, and Manon's face too from all those old photos at the manor. I thought for sure it was him – that's why I stayed where I landed, partly because I trusted him to take me to a ranger station, which he did, but also because I didn't want to lose him. I wanted to bring him to you so you could meet him…"

"Thank you, Tristan, but you didn't have to do that," Charlemagne replied to him. "I have the Protection Squad investigating the matter and we had tracked someone around the age of eighteen who would be in these parts. I had a plan in place already, but between this forest fire, the media, and all sorts of unpredictabilities… I am thankful nonetheless for your efforts."

"I'm not done," Tristan replied, "so after I couldn't return to you at the ranger station at Whitelee, I stayed with who I thought to be your son and I learned more about him… the more I learned, the more sure I was, but then I discovered an inconvenient belief of his. Charles, he's a far-right extremist, an eco-fascist – but you probably already know that by now if you heard about what happened, and I tried to stop it… I told him we'd go to the gas plant and look for some information, thinking it was a Cabernet facility, but it wasn't and we almost got caught. I didn't know it, but he planted some explosives while we were separated, and he let them off to mask our escape. Only afterwards, I realized that he wasn't your son, Charles, he's the son of some man named Cunningham, the owner of Cunningham Industries."

"Aidan Cunningham?" Charlemagne questioned.

"Yes."

"I only found out less than a couple hours ago, and I felt so stupid… because I thought he was him! I thought he was your son, because he looks like you, acts like you sometimes, has weird interests like you – Charles, it's weird and sometimes disturbing how similar he is to you even though you two never met, but it was all a lie, and now I don't know where he's going or what he's planning. I'm scared for him, especially since we're now both wanted."

"Tristan, take it easy," Charlemagne cautioned. "You did well, but it's time to come back with me – the two of you. I'm going to see what can be done about getting us out of here before they identify you, if they'll be able to do that, and we're going to return to Canada."

"I didn't want to abandon him – it still feels wrong to abandon him even though he's not your son," Tristan cried out. "I thought I could change him and that I was changing him, but then he betrayed me and I'm confused."

"Terror bombing and the targeting of civilian populations is never okay, even at times of war," Charlemagne stated. "The Second World War is a testament of that cruel reality, and Finn is wrong to hold such beliefs of his… Only Bolsheviks pursue and adopt violence to advance their beliefs…"

"I don't want him to get in trouble," Tristan complained. "I don't want him to go to jail. I want to help him see right and be happy, but… he's not happy and he won't ever see right. I don't see any point anymore, especially since he's not your son."

"Tristan, the boy you described and are with *is* my son," Charlemagne revealed. "I've reviewed the entire case Mr. Heavner was overseeing for me, and the boy that they had pointed to is the boy I saw with you at the natural gas facility. Your instincts didn't deceive you. Your mind deceived you most likely out of shock from what happened. Rest easy, we're going home…"

"Finn too?" Tristan questioned.

Yes," Charlemagne responded, "although it won't be easy, I'm going to ensure that he gets the best legal representation possible, but it will be difficult."

"He'll never agree to come," Tristan said.

"Let me talk to him, "Charlemagne replied.

"I don't want him to get in trouble. If he gets in trouble, I'll get in trouble and I don't want to get in trouble. I don't want to do time."

Tristan brought his hands to his face and then looked to Charlemagne.

"Can't you get both of us an escape route? A way out of the country without going through customs and immigration? Isn't there a back route? Can't we contact the GDP?"

"Tristan…."

"What do you have planned? Anything?"

"I've been focusing on getting you out of the forest," Charlemagne scolded, "so please, come with me."

Tristan looked at Charlemagne. He then looked back towards the forest and to the camp.

"He won't agree to come," Tristan said to Charlemagne again. "You don't understand him. He doesn't want to anything to do with modern life… all he knows is violence."

Charlemagne looked to Tristan.

"You need to leave him here, I think," Tristan said. "I'm sorry, especially since he's your son, but he won't come with us… not unless he can be convinced, and that's something that won't happen…"

Tristan felt a tear come down his eye.

"Can I go say goodbye to him?" Tristan questioned. "Alone? I promise I'll return."

Charlemagne sighed.

"Are you sure he can't be convinced? Can I speak with him?" Charlemagne asked.

"Not now," Tristan replied. "I'm sorry – he's your son and it sucks that this is how it is… but I'll talk to him before I leave. How about that?"

Charlemagne looked to Tristan. He gave him the flashlight in his hand.

"We'll be waiting here," Charlemagne said. "Take as much time as you need."

Tristan nodded. He took the flashlight and left. Charlemagne watched as Tristan went into the forest with the light guiding him. Tristan went through the forest and shined his light around to make sure he was going the right direction. He eventually returned to the camp and rushed over to Finn.

"Finn! Finn!" Tristan said, waking him.

Finn groaned in his sleep.

"What?" Finn questioned.

"We need to go," Tristan said to him. "I heard some movement up ahead and think the Feds are on to us."

Finn's eyes opened wide. He got out and put his shoes on. He then quickly put his sleeping bag away.

"Pull the tent apart – we need to leave," Finn stated in a rush.

Tristan went to the tent and pulled it apart. The two quickly disassembled the camp and threw their stuff between their two packs. Tristan wrote in the dirt with his finger as they were busy. Once it was all set, Finn looked to Tristan.

"Thank you," Finn said to him.

"Yeah," Tristan replied, nodding. "Come on, let's move."

The two went into the forest and walked a short distance before coming to a rocky creek.

"Let's head on down this way," Tristan suggested. "It'll conceal our footsteps."

"Nice idea," Finn replied, following him.

The two walked along the water with Tristan's flashlight guiding them. Together, they disappeared away, travelling southwards and away from Charlemagne.

Act 5, Scene 4

Charlemagne and Miklos waited by the river stream for Tristan to return. Five minutes had passed, and Charlemagne looked content. Ten minutes had passed, and he let out a sigh. Twenty minutes, and he looked to his team. At thirty minutes passed, he looked to Miklos.

"Right, I've had enough – it doesn't take that long to say farewell to someone," Charlemagne stated. "Come on."

Charlemagne led the way with Miklos and Lukas aiming flashlights. The two came to where the camp was and Charlemagne looked in horror. He pointed to a spec of dirt and saw a message written, 'I'm sorry.'

"Dammit!" Charlemagne cursed. "Tristan!" he screamed, letting of an echo. "Tristan!"

"I have footprints here," Miklos said, pointing to the edge of the clearing.

"Follow them!" Charlemagne ordered. "Find him!"

Miklos led the way into the forest with Lukas. The two aimed their flashlights at the ground, pointing out footprints that led to a river. Once there, they examined the other side for a continuing track of prints.

"Where did they go? Do you see?" Lukas questioned.

The other mercenaries with them produced their own flashlights and together they all searched around while Charlemagne brought a hand to his sweaty head. He looked around and around, with a worried expression upon his face and eyes that seemed as if they were about to cry. He looked around and then down the stream, southbound, and brought a hand to his mouth. He stared down the river with angry eyes.

The mercenaries had spread out and covered a large portion of earth together, but none could find any tracks, and in fairness, there were none to find.

"Down the river!" Charlemagne shouted. "Hurry!"

"Are you sure?!" Miklos questioned, pointing his flashlight to him.

"Yes! Quickly!" Charlemagne rushed, motioning them forward.

The mercenaries went to the river and proceeded downstream. They ran and kept their flashlights forward and side to side. Charlemagne ran with them and they went a fair distance before reaching a small waterfall that went downwards. Miklos shined his light over the waterfall while Charlemagne pushed himself to the front of the crowd. He looked down and around.

"There is no sight of them," Miklos reported. "What do you want us to do? Retrace our steps?"

Charlemagne looked down the waterfall with bitter eyes. His fists were enclosed and he looked tense.

"No," Charlemagne replied. "Who knows how long of a start they have ahead of us and where they've gone. They know we're on their trail and have attempted to outsmart us, but your men are tired and exhausted. Contact the helicopter and let's return to the ranger station to reorganize."

"Yes, Charles," Miklos replied, taking out his satellite radio. "Delta-One, this is Charlie-One in need of exfil at my coordinates…"

. . .

The light helicopter took the team away from Wauchope Forest and back to Butterburn. Charlemagne looked at his watch and saw that it was well into three o'clock in the morning when they returned. The helicopter set down at the helipad and Charlemagne bid the team farewell as they went to their tents near the helipad. Miklos stayed with Charlemagne and walked with him to the warden station.

The two walked up the steps of the house and then entered inside. Once Miklos closed the door behind him, Charlemagne brought his hands to his face.

"I can't believe it!" Charlemagne shouted. "What is wrong with him?! How could I trust him again! How can I ever trust him ever again?!"

Diana woke up at the sound of Charlemagne yelling downstairs.

"Please, Charles," Miklos replied, motioning him to come into the learning hub and away from the foyer.

Charlemagne complied and walked with him.

"Why didn't he stay where he landed after he fell from the boat?! Why?!"

"With all due respect, Charles, he is a teenager," Miklos said with a sigh. "You should expect this behavior from him."

"A teenager? Not once – not once has Tristan ever acted like a self-centered adolescent!" Charlemagne remarked. "I respected him for his maturity, but this! There is no logic towards his behavior!"

Diana came out of bed upon hearing Tristan's name. She put on some running shoes and grabbed a hoodie before going downstairs and stopping by the locked door between the private and public space. She gently opened the door and entered the foyer, standing outside of the learning hub to eavesdrop.

"His behavior, and my idiocy to trust him! I should never have told him about my son! I should have kept my mouth quiet, but because he trusted me with his own secret – a large one at that, I had the gall to trust him with mine! What a fool I've been!" Charlemagne lamented. "Oh, what a fool I was to think that he would understand!"

Charlemagne proceeded to pace around the foyer.

"What a situation this has become, Tristan and my own biological son, wanted by the British authorities on charges of terrorism!" Charlemagne remarked. "What am I to do, Miklos?"

"Get some rest, please," Miklos insisted. "You are tired. I am tired. You need to have some rest!"

"How can I rest with the emotions inside me?! My biological son and my adopted son, both equally my own children, lost out there as two-thirds of the world burns, one lost because of a set of beliefs that arose out my lack of presence in his life, and the other lost out there because of his own set of beliefs that he needs to do good for my benefit – both beliefs of my own mistakes! Did you hear what he said? He said he was only with Finn because he thought he was my son. If I hadn't brought us to this accursed forest, I would never have lost him! I should never have involved him in my personal crusade! I should have remained alone, just as I have for the last months – alone to deal with my issues in this search for him, and now that I've found him – all has gone to hell!"

Diana frowned. She moved around the side and presented herself.

"That's why we're here? Because of your biological son?!" Diana questioned.

"Diana, please," Charlemagne replied, lowering his tone and looking to her with tired eyes. "Not now."

"I thought you left because of Judith's death. I thought you left to give speeches and inspire people. I thought you brought us here to admire nature and enjoy the outdoors, but all this time, it was never about Judith, or the speeches, or about the nature, but about you and your son," Diana accused, eyes watering, "because of you, Tristan is now lost with some stranger, accused of terrorism and I might never get to see him again?!"

Charlemagne didn't respond.

"How could you do that?!" Diana questioned. "How could you be so selfish?!"

"Diana…" Charlemagne replied.

"Yes, Diana," Miklos said, moving towards her, "please."

Miklos attempted to move her out of the room.

"No!" Diana shouted, moving away from him. "I thought we were staying here to bring Cabernet Industries to justice, but I suppose that was a lie too. You placed Tristan's life on the line for your own personal quest – to find your son, and in the process, you've cost the life of your other son. The boy that admires you so much, and unlike any other boy – an admiration that equates the admiration you had for your grandfather… Tristan was the only person I had left in my life… How could you?"

Diana's held a cascade of tears at her eyes. She wiped them.

"Find him," Diana commanded. "Find him and bring him right back to us… whatever it takes, and you alleviate whatever charges he might be facing, whatever responsibility he is being asked to take from the government, and you set things right."

Charlemagne looked at her with guilt. His own eyes seemed as though they might cry. He nodded to her.

"Yes, Diana," Charlemagne replied. "I will. I promise you. I will do whatever I can to bring Tristan back…"

Diana looked at Charlemagne for half a minute before looking to Miklos. She left on her own and returned to the foyer, attempting to enter the private area, but not being let in. She instead stayed by the door to cry while the adults looked to each other with sentiment.

"Why don't you get some sleep...?" Charlemagne said to Miklos. "I'll make phone calls in the morning and begin to work on some sort of solution. In the meantime, I need to attend to Diana and be sure that she's okay."

The two listened to the tears of Diana. Miklos didn't object. He took one step towards the exit, but then looked to Charlemagne. He walked towards him.

"You know, she loves him, right?" Miklos said to him in a quiet tone.

Charlemagne nodded.

"I know."

Act 5, Scene 5

Tristan shot an arrow towards a tree, hitting it the in the middle of the trunk. He stood approximately ten meters from the target, at the other side of a clearing in the woods. Two days had passed since Charlemagne had seen Tristan and in that time, a heat wave had fallen upon the forest and brought on temperatures of more than thirty degrees Celsius. The sun was blazing down and Tristan was dressed in his shorts and hiking shoes, while his shirt dried out from being washed.

Once Tristan had run out of arrows, he lowered the bow and walked over to the tree to collect the various arrows all around. He placed them in the two bags and then came back to where he was stood, sitting down at a tree and wiping the sweat from his forehead. He looked up to the clear sky and then stood up, taking both bags with him to the camp.

A light wind trailed through the forest, brushing at the deciduous trees of Kielder Forest as he walked back. A large fire burned in the fire pit at the center of the camp. The tent was up. The boys had established a camp at the top of a short hill atop of a beach to a large river below where Finn was in the water, just up to his knees, with a makeshift spear in his hand. He threw the spear into the water, pulling it out as he attempted to spearfish.

Tristan unloaded the longbow and bags of arrows and proceeded to make his way to the beach below. He looked over to Finn as he continued to attempt to fish.

"Catch anything?" Tristan questioned.

"Not yet," Finn replied, looking to him. "It's not as easy as it looks."

Tristan took off his shoes and stepped into the cool water. He made his way over to Finn and took the spear. He then looked into the clear water as he saw some moderate-sized fish swimming about. Tristan attempted to spear the fish but was unsuccessful. The fish ran away from him.

Finn crossed his arms. Tristan aimed the spear at another one nearby. He launched the spear and missed again. Tristan groaned.

"The problem is the damn refraction," Tristan complained. "I told you we should have made a makeshift fishing pole!"

"Give me that," Finn said, taking the spear. "You're worse than me. You're supposed to avoid casting your shadow over them."

Finn aimed the spear and looked over to a fish. He aimed and brought the spear into the water, jabbing a fish in the side.

"Haha!" Finn cheered. "You see?"

"Whatever," Tristan replied, crossing his arms.

Finn pulled the fish out and showed Tristan his catch. The fish was medium-sized and flapping its tail around. Tristan looked at it and got a closer look at Finn's makeshift trident spear. Once Tristan was done admiring the fish, Finn walked to the coast with it.

"Come on, I'll let you gut him and set him to cook," Finn said, turning back to Tristan in the water.

"Yeah, I'll catch up with you – I need to have a bath before we leave," Tristan replied.

"Suit yourself," Finn responded, going uphill with the fish.

Tristan stayed in the water and bathed himself in the water before resting on the beach to dry. Once he was set, he returned to the camp where Finn was by the fire, fiddling with some sort of device. Tristan looked at the device in his hand – it looked similar to the satellite radio that Miklos carried with him.

"What's that?" Tristan questioned, sitting down next to him.

"Nothing," Finn replied. "What took you so long?"

"I was sunbathing," Tristan stated. "What are you hiding from me?"

"Nothing," Finn insisted.

"Don't keep secrets from me," Tristan complained, taking his breakfast and starting to eat.

"I was contacting someone!" Finn yelled. "I have a plan and needed some supplies. Happy?"

"What plan?"

"Never you mind," Finn replied.

"I thought we were going north – to hide," Tristan said to him, stopping from eating. "At least until all of this heat around us dies down and we can return to our normal lives."

"I know," Finn responded, annoyed, "but this is important... My father is going to be at our summer home at Kielder Lake tomorrow, and... I have to take care of him."

"What does that mean? Kill him?"

Finn didn't respond.

"You idiot!" Tristan yelled, slapping him in the shoulder. "We're in big enough trouble as it is and you want to kill someone? Your own father?

"I'm doing the world a favor! The death of one terrible man can make the world a better place!" Finn argued. "You need to let me do this! I'm going to do it whether you let me or not!"

"It's not like I can run to the cops and stop you!" Tristan replied. "Please, Finn, don't do this – Leave him alone! Start a new life!"

"I have no life..."

Tristan shook his head. Finn stood up and left.

"I'm going to bathe," Finn stated. "If you need me, I'll be down at the river. Your clothes are dry. We'll leave when I get back..."

Tristan watched Finn as he left. Tristan ate a bit of his food and then left the rest aside. He held an anxious face and brought his hands to his head. He looked miserable.

· · ·

Later in the day, Finn and Tristan packed up their camp and left to hike towards Kielder Lake in the south. The two stopped near some bushes and looked at some berries. Finn held a small guide in his hand as the two looked at the plant in question. The plant had dark red berries pointed up from small stems branching from a thin stem. The plant also had sailboat-shaped leaves that were small.

"Looks like baneberries," Finn remarked, pointing at a picture. "They're poisonous..."

"Damn," Tristan replied. "Okay."

The two continued to walk from the bush and continued along through the forest. The two of them were dressed in their typical clothing.

"If we reach a field, I'll look for some dandelions. I read that they can be boiled and are rich in vitamins," Finn said. "Also, spruce needles make a nice tea that's rich in vitamin C. You can also chew the needles to get those nice vitamins that we need."

The boys continued to walk along the forest. There was a light haze from the forest fire above them and the skies were yellowish as the sun began to set. Finn looked at his map, which was folded to show their immediate area. They walked for another ten minutes before reaching a clearing between the forest of tall grass. In the middle of the clearing was some sort of container underneath a parachute.

Finn walked to the object and removed the parachute, pushing it back and opening the reinforced container below.

Tristan looked inside with horror at what was inside. Inside the container was a rifle, set with various magazines of ammunition. Finn picked up the rifle and examined the gun. He then looked to Tristan. The two didn't speak. Tristan held an upset face and left to stand back at the forest, waiting for Finn to return. He watched as Finn re-arranged the items in his backpack before returning to him.

The two continued to trek through the forest, reaching the top of a hill that looked out and towards a road past a field, and behind the road was a layer of grass before the large lake. Kielder Lake was half a kilometer in length and stretched for more than a kilometer in width. The surface of the lake was clear and reflected the area around it. Beyond the lake was a large, thick cloud of grey smoke over the entire forest on the opposite side. The trees consisted primarily of coniferous trees and were tall and dense.

At the base of the lake below them, to the right, in the distance, was a lakeside resort almost four-stories tall. The structure was large and long and had various balconies and a marvelous garden set with a swimming pool in the back. The garden went to a lakeside pathway, which then led to two docks over the water. On the left, further along, was a three story home at the end of a dirt road that sprouted from the main road. The house was slightly hidden by trees surrounding the house. All around the lake, dotted across the large frontier of the beach were various homes each with their own docks in different forms.

"I'm going to set a camp nearby," Finn stated. "I'm where I need to be."

The two walked back into the forest and established a camp by a small creek. They ate supper and kept to themselves. Tristan stayed by the fire, while Finn was at a clearing by a hill. Tristan was throwing scraps into the fire, seeing them burn. He gave a lonely sigh and decided to stand up. He walked away from the camp and went out to the clearing where Finn was lying on the grass, looking up to the star-filled sky on his own.

Tristan walked over to him and looked at him with pity and sadness. Finn had his arms behind his head and seemed at peace. His flannel shirt was unbuttoned and he wasn't wearing his tank top. He had his shorts on, but was bare foot.

"Aren't they wonderful? The stars?" Finn questioned.

"Yeah..." Tristan replied. "They are."

Tristan got down and brought himself to lie down next to Finn. He looked up to the bountiful sky with all the stars past the smoky haze. The moon was full and shining down and there was an equal level of light, dark, but not too dark; lit, but not too lit.

"People have forgotten their roots and their nature," Finn stated. "They've become incorporated into the liberal democratic world and have lost their greater sense of identity within their race, their greater family: the people who have shared centuries of blood and hardship together only to meet a demise worse than death out of their self-destruction."

Finn sighed.

"Do you know why I need to do this? You say to me, be peaceful, but I cannot... I cannot sit idle while my family is violated. By our ancestors, generations upon generations, we became rooted like the tree in the forest, and people like my father represents the elites who wish to root out the forest. He is an oligarch; a plutocrat; a slave owner. All he cares about is power and money, and by eliminating him, I can take down the evil that I hate so much."

Finn went quiet.

"All these years of suffering alone have both taught me to be and made me strong, and being in these forests not only provides me refuge, but gives me strength through the divine to push on forward – a gentle reminder of what there is to lose as much as when I look into the eyes of an innocent white child. We need to be strong for them, Tristan. We need to be strong so that we can defend that which we love from those that threaten. As long as their blood is spilt, I will be there and the firestorm will intensify and rage on to purify the bane that society drowns in. I am only defending that which I love, my folk, all the white children, this forest, you... You're the only friend I have. You're my best friend. I want the best for everyone, even other families, but even then my principle concern is my own, and is that wrong? No, it is natural – it is what natural law dictates because mother nature is a fascist."

Tristan continued looking up to the sky with a serious face. He didn't say anything. Finn went quiet again.

"Can I tell you something else?" Finn asked.

"What?" Tristan replied.

"I like wolves," Finn said, "which is funny, because when I was a child, nothing – absolutely nothing scared me more than the depiction of a werewolf, but now, the thought of a werewolf settles me. A man who at dark turns into the beast of a wolf, murderous and ravenous, but that is not all that a wolf is. Yes, a wolf represents savagery, but a wolf is also a warrior. A wolf is brave. A wolf is loyal. A wolf protects that which he loves. A wolf is fierce. A wolf is always willing to do what is necessary, and I, Tristan, am a wolf."

Finn took a deep breath and sat up.

"I am a wolf in hallowed places, alone on his own in this greater Earth, and I will defend that which I love to the bitter end... even if I will continue to be alone, suffering as I always will continue to suffer..."

Finn tilted his head up to look at the moon. He then howled loudly. Tristan listened to the howl. It was a sad howl. He remained quiet for a couple minutes before looking to Tristan. "Thanks for staying with me," Finn stated. "I appreciate it." Tristan closed his eyes and took slow, careful breaths.

"You've been nothing but truthful to me, Finn," Tristan said in a nervous voice, "but now I have to honest with you."

"Two nights ago, I spoke with my guardian. He and his men had found me – this was the night when I woke you. He offered me a chance to return home, but I didn't go with him. And before you think it was because I wanted to be with you, yes and no, the real reason was because I was scared to get arrested for what happened at the gas plant."

"You weren't identified though... I was," Finn replied. "You could have left, returned to Canada, and that would have been it."

"I didn't trust you though... I didn't trust you to not get caught and rat me out, especially if I left unannounced..."

"You're scared of me? You think I'd sell you out if I got caught (not that I would get caught)!" Finn said with a sense of betrayal before settling down. "I... I wouldn't do that to you, Tristan... I wouldn't."

"How can I not be scared of you? You're merciless! You detonated a bomb that injured dozens of people, and you seem to have no remorse or actual regret! Tomorrow, you plan to kill the man that raised you, because... because you have some sort of vendetta against him... some sort of moral qualm..."

"You- you don't know what I feel," Finn replied to him. "You don't know the burden I take! You don't know that this *isn't* personal or even just business – it's war...!" he shouted, taking a deep breath before looking aside. "I'm sorry," he apologized in a calmer voice.

"But this was two days ago, and even though I am still skeptical of you..." Tristan said, swallowing his breath. "I want you to know that you *are* my best friend and that I'm here now because I don't want to abandon you so that you'd be on your own."

Finn looked back at him and said, "So, that's it then – it's pity."

"No," Tristan denied, "it's not that. Why are you making this so difficult? I'm here because... because in a sense, you're my brother."

"So, it's because you think I'm the biological son of your guardian? A man I have never met or intend to meet."

"No, it's not that either – God!" Tristan shouted, looking aside and standing up.

Tristan brought a hand to his hair and sighed.

"I'm here because I care about you, Finn," Tristan said with clarity. "I care about you, and I don't want you to ruin your life (any more than it has been ruined). Please, listen to me," he added, turning and kneeling down. "We do not have to live like this... as outlaws in this forest. You can come with me, start a new life in Canada, and escape this old life. If you really care about your people, about this forest and forests alike, about me... then come to Canada than stay here..."

Finn looked at him with a serious face. He looked to the side, took a deep breath, and then looked back to Tristan.

"I... I can't stay here anymore though, Finn... I miss my girlfriend... I miss my guardian... I miss my life, and I want to offer you the chance to be a part of that and start anew. It can happen..."

Finn looked at him and then left. Tristan watched him leave and sat down, tears falling from his eyes. He stayed atop of the hill and cried. He wiped his eyes with his hands and then stood up. He returned to the camp and saw the fire continuing to run. Finn had taken his sleeping bag and laid it out across from the tent. He was already inside, laying on his side, and asleep.

Tristan looked at him and put out the fire. He then climbed into the tent and wrapped himself with blankets. He shivered as he tried to sleep, closing his eyes and looking to Finn as he lay on his side with view of him. He opened his eyes again to see Finn where he was. He then closed them and drifted off to a deep sleep.

Act 6, Scene 1

Tristan woke up the following morning in the exact same position having not woken up at all throughout the night. He looked over to where Finn's sleeping bag was and took a sigh of relief that it looked as though he was still in bed. Tristan closed his eyes again and then stretched out. He pushed the blankets back and got out of the tent, standing up and looking over to Finn. He then turned his face as he looked at the sleeping bag.

The sleeping bag had an odd form to it. Tristan went over and realized that Finn was gone. The inside of the sleeping bag had been stuffed with his backpack and various items that were inside. Among them was a letter with Tristan's name written in the front with a black marker. Tristan took the letter and opened it.

'Tristan, I'm sorry about last night and the fight we had, and I'm sorry you believed that I would rat you out if you left me. I wouldn't. Please, return to your family and your girlfriend, and fill this world with many White children. I respect your decision to not help me, so please respect mine. Both our fates and actions will lead to a better existence for the future of the White race – Finn.'

"No," Tristan complained, crumpling the letter. "Finn!" he shouted.

Tristan took a step away from the camp before taking a step back. He looked around and quickly scavenged the longbow and a bag of arrows, tying it around his belt. He then put on his hiking shoes and his brown t-shirt before he dashed off and went into the forest. Tristan armed the bow and continued to run without stop, going past the trees and bushes, and jumping over every log and stuck out root. He came to a hill and looked down and over to the lake.

Across the lake he could see the forest fire awake and alive, arriving to Kielder Lake as it consumed the forest on the other side and sent a large cloud of dark smoke upwards and towards where Tristan was, mixing the cloudless blue skies behind with the torment ahead.

Tristan's head jerked over towards the large lakeside lodge to the left as he heard shots fired. He immediately set foot down the hill before him and crossed the green field to each the road. From here, he ran down and went towards dirt road behind the small forest of deciduous trees around the property.

The gate of the estate was wide open for him to rush through and make his approach to the house ahead. Tristan looked ahead. The Cunningham summer home had the appearance of an English countryside house set with stone foundations, wooden exterior walls and blackish-blue shingles on the rooftops. The roof was set in the style of a hip roof with dormer windows also with hip roofs. The frames of the window were white and in a Georgian style, crossed.

The front of the house had a gravel causeway in the shape of a circle that wrapped around and was behind a stone wall the separated the trees of the surrounding forest from the front garden. The space that did not have gravel consisted of mowed grass, and at the center of the causeway was a stone statue. There were bushes in front of the house and several cars parked at the sides of the entrance.

Tristan fastened his pace as he heard screams come from the home as well as further gunshots. He soon discovered that the house was larger, wider than he originally thought it was as he arrived past the stone walls and came to the driveway.

Upon his arrival, Tristan immediately saw that there was nobody to be seen. He looked around for a brief moment before going towards the front door, which had been left open. He entered the home and could hear another set of screams come from somewhere within the house.

"Finn!" Tristan shouted.

The foyer of the home was larger than that of the Cabernet Manor and more heavily decorated. The entrance of the house had a set of stairs on either side of the mid-section that went up to a second-floor gallery. The walls and floor consisted of mahogany wood, carved and elegant with beams across the ceiling. The foyer was heavily decorated, and at the left-side was a developing fire rising upwards and spreading. Tristan looked at it.

At the sound of some gunfire, Tristan saw some men and women in business suits run from ahead and come towards Tristan, stopping in front of him, but then rushing past him as he simply looked at them with stupor.

Tristan passed them and came to a corridor past the hallway and stairs. The corridor went down on either side for him to follow. He looked at the other direction from where the people had come from, pointing his arrow in preparation of seeing Finn, and then going back the way the business people had come. He went forward and stopped at either open door of each room, looking inside only to see them without anyone inside. He then came to the room at the end of the hallway, which was through a French window.

The room appeared to be some sort of press conference room with chairs in two sections between an aisle and red carpet that went to a podium. Behind the podium were Georgian windows that looked out to the forest behind. Above the podium was a balcony overhead.

Tristan entered the room and was immediately grabbed, forced against a wall and restrained by a man in a black suit.

"Hey, what gives!" Tristan complained, struggling.

Tristan elbowed the man in the side. He was wearing some sort of body armor. Tristan then decided to headbutt the man, grabbing a vase nearby and throwing it towards him.

"I don't want to hurt you!" Tristan shouted.

The man went towards him again. Tristan quickly took an arrow from his bag and shot it towards the man's leg. The arrow was shot into the thigh causing the man to yell out and scream as he fell to the floor.

Tristan looked at him with regret. He then jerked his neck towards the balcony as another man, this one with a handgun aimed it towards Tristan. Tristan took another arrow and shot it to the man, hitting him in the shoulder and causing the firearm to go off and land on the floor below. The man coincidentally fell to the side and grabbed his shoulder. Tristan then heard the rifle go off, but at a closer proximately to when he last heard it.

From the press conference room, Tristan went forward and towards the door on the left as the one on the right had a 'Fire Exit' sign on the front. Tristan came to a long library and looked ahead, up the balcony ahead of him to where he saw Finn above, firing his rifle to the left of Tristan and into a room on the other side.

Finn was dressed in an entirely different set of clothes. He was dressed in a beige tactical suit with a vest that held magazines of ammunition. He held the rifle he had collected yesterday and at his face was a type of bandana or mask that covered his neck and up to his jawbone and over the nose. The mask was black and had the white imprint of the lower half portion of a skull set with a pair of teeth that contained sharpened incisor teeth like fangs. Finn's hair was free and as long as it was when he first met him. He didn't wear a helmet.

"Finn!" Tristan shouted, readying an arrow and aiming the bow towards him.

Finn turned to Tristan and looked at him. He then pointed his rifle towards him, aiming it. Tristan shot the arrow before jumping out of the way and behind a bookcase to his left as Finn took shots at him.

"Leave!" Finn yelled back. "I told you to go home!"

Tristan peaked out from around the corner to see Finn scanning the ground below for Tristan. He sneaked around to the other side and went down the aisle to the left-side of the library, underneath the balcony below and coming to the corner to see Finn above. He shot another arrow towards him, missing him and hitting the wooden railing. Finn jerked over and shot his gun towards where Tristan was, but Tristan had sneaked off and was below him.

A ladder provided access to the balcony above, but Tristan instead went behind and up a set of stairs that wrapped around and came to the second floor. Finn turned to him as he saw and heard Tristan run towards him. Tristan shot an arrow towards the rifle. Finn flinched. Tristan rushed towards him and grabbed both his wrists, causing the rifle at his hands to hang by its sling from his neck.

The two struggled as Tristan pushed him towards the railing. Finn overpowered Tristan and pushed him back. Finn then went towards him, grabbed him, and pulled him over the railing so that he fell to the ground. Tristan's body slammed onto the floor. He quickly recovered and grabbed the longbow, running up the stairs and reaching the top where Finn had closed a set of doors, barricading them somehow for him to be unable to get through. Tristan went back downstairs and towards the ladder that was available, but Finn had also set a fire that outright prevented him from following from this side.

Tristan looked down the aisle and saw another ladder at the end. He ran towards this ladder and climbed up it, reaching the top and looking to the fast-spread of the fire before opening the doors in front that went into the same wide corridor on the other side. Tristan looked to the right and then the left.

The fire that started in the foyer had spread and affected the left wall. Tristan entered this middle corridor as he heard gunshots and Finn ahead, firing towards some business executives. The executives ran off with the aid of some bodyguards into a room at the end of the corridor.

Tristan sprinted down the corridor and towards Finn. Finn turned around and pointed the rifle towards him. Tristan pointed the rifle up and tackled Finn onto the ground, getting on top of him. The two struggled again as Tristan attempted to restrain him and Finn thrashed him off.

"Stop!" Tristan yelled at Finn. "Please, stop!"

"Get off me!" Finn cried out.

Embers spilled downwards around them as the fire spread to the beams of the ceiling above. The two heard the creaks of wood followed by a slump. The floor fell by a foot before giving up entirely. Tristan was forced to let go of Finn as the two slid down and fell to the ground floor, entering the main corridor in front of the main foyer.

The boys separated as they rolled at their landing. Tristan got up onto a knee and looked to Finn who was on his back. Finn was looking across the hallway with vengeful eyes.

"Father!" Finn shouted.

Tristan looked and saw an elderly businessman protected by two bodyguards in black suits. The elderly gentleman, Aidan Cunningham, had thin grey hair atop of his head, a squared jawline and blue eyes. He had ears that stuck out and was below average height.

"Get me out of here," Aidan commanded his men as they produced pistols from their suits.

The bodyguards pointed their guns towards the two of them. Finn aimed his rifle towards his father. Tristan picked up the longbow.

"No!" Tristan yelled back, taking an arrow and firing at one of the guards.

Tristan hit a guard in the thigh, causing him to fall to the floor while the other took Mr. Cunningham to the ground and fired at Finn. Tristan took another arrow and shot it towards the other guard, hitting him in the thigh. The arrow didn't cause him to fall over as with others, but did cause him to cry out in pain. Finn attempted to shoot from his own rifle, but the rifle simply clicked. He rolled off from the ground and moved out of the way to change magazines.

"Get *me* out of here!" Mr. Cunningham complained.

The guard allowed him to stand and the two rushed back and away, down the hall. The guard walked with a limp. Finn set off after him once his gun was reloaded. Tristan went off after Finn. Finn pushed Tristan aside, into a wall to get an advantage over him. Tristan slammed into the wall and Finn opened fire towards his father as they came to the end of the corridor. They lowered their heads and then rushed to the right.

Tristan pounced towards Finn, grabbing the rifle and pushing him towards the wall. Finn slapped his arm into Tristan's face and then kicked him back. Tristan fell to the floor. Finn attempted to escape, but Tristan grabbed him by the ankle, causing him to fall over. Tristan then slammed his body into his to attempt to restrain him.

In the ambience of the crackle of wood and fire, Tristan and Finn could both here sirens. Finn grabbed Tristan by the throat and proceeded to choke him. He pushed him back and brought him to the floor, pressing down at his throat. Tristan grabbed Finn's wrists and clenched his teeth. His face was red. Finn landed a punch to Tristan's face and eased his grip. Tristan laid his head to the side. Finn punched him again, causing Tristan's nose to bleed. Once he was done, he stood up and began to leave after his father.

Tristan lay on his back and moved his head, looking around to the fire that surrounded them. He then looked to the left, towards the entrance as he saw police vehicles at the front of the house with police officers in blue tactical uniforms with assault rifles. Tristan brought a hand to his head and another to the ground to help him up. Tristan stood up and grabbed the longbow. He then proceeded to walk down the hall and go the way that Mr. Cunningham had went.

At the end of the hall, Tristan came to a stairwell that went up to the second-floor of the mansion. On the second-floor, to the left was the corridor that the two had fallen down from. The fire continued to spread and it seemed as though where they were, were the last safe places. To the right was an open set of doors that went into an elegant study, far larger than Charlemagne's and of course, more decorated with an assortment of portraits, mementos, artefacts, and a grizzly bear skin rug.

Tristan looked inside and saw Finn with his father on the ground, on his side in front of his large red wooden desk. Finn stood over him, a leg at either side. He landed a punch to the side of his father's face. The security guard who had taken an arrow to the thigh was against a wall, near a fireplace on the left, unconscious in a pool of his own blood. Tristan looked to Finn and took an arrow from his bag. He readied it and shot towards Finn.

The arrow hit the desk and forced Finn to let go of his father. Finn looked to Tristan annoyed. He picked up his rifle and pointed it to Tristan.

"Go away!" Finn shouted, stepping over his father and walking to Tristan. "I will shoot you!"

Mr. Cunningham proceeded to crawl away as soon as he was behind Finn. He moved slowly.

"Shoot me then," Tristan replied.

Finn looked at Tristan with a sharp eye. He lowered his rifle and shot at Tristan's feet. Tristan flinched but kept his distance between himself and Finn. Finn growled and threw his rifle off.

"I won't shoot you, but you won't shoot me!" Finn yelled, charging towards him.

Tristan lowered the bow as Finn tackled him to the ground. Finn punched him in the face again. Tristan grabbed his wrist, but Finn broke free and attempted to punch him again.

"The police are here – it's over..." Tristan stated in a broken voice. "I'm sorry."

"You ruined everything!" Finn shouted, punching him again. "I hate you!"

Finn punched him once more. Tristan looked at him with regret and then past him as he saw Mr. Cunningham, grabbing his side, with a pistol in his hand as he stood in front of his desk with blood drooping from his mouth.

Tristan wrapped his arms around Finn, hugged him and brought him close as Mr. Cunningham let out a loud shot from his revolver. The shot missed them. Tristan pushed Finn away from him and then rolled to the side, taking cover. Finn took cover at the other side, picking up the long bow. Another shot fired. Tristan attempted to step out but stepped back as a third shot fired towards him.

"Pass me an arrow!" Finn asked, motioning his hand.

"Come out, you spoiled brat!" Mr. Cunningham yelled, taking a fourth shot as Tristan threw an arrow from his bag.

Mr. Cunningham shot his fifth and sixth shot close to Finn's feet, grazing his thigh. At the seventh pull of the trigger, the revolver clicked. At this moment, Finn stepped out and shot an arrow towards Mr. Cunningham, hitting him in the shoulder. He yelled out and dropped the gun.

Once he was done, he brought the bow around his shoulder and went over to grab his rifle. He pointed it towards Mr. Cunningham.

"Please, Finn..." Tristan begged, stepping into the room, "... don't..."

"Why not!" Finn shouted at him. "Why shouldn't I? Give me on good reason why this worthless soul shouldn't live...!"

"It's not about that..." Tristan replied. "Lives aren't ours to take!"

Finn shook his head.

"Please..." Mr. Cunningham said in a weak voice. "Please don't kill me."

"Shut up!" Finn replied to him, looking out a window. "We're leaving – on your feet!"

Mr. Cunningham stood up and raised his arms. He pointed him forward and led him away from the study.

"You too!" Finn shouted. "You're coming with us..."

"You won't shoot me..." Tristan replied.

"No, but I'll shoot him, for whatever reason that matters to you."

Tristan looked back at him and he walked out. Finn led them downstairs and stopped in the corridor below.

"Freeze! Drop the weapon!" a team of tactical police officers shouted.

Finn jumped and took his father by the neck, pointing the rifle and using his father as a shield.

"I'll shoot him!" Finn yelled. "Back off!"

Tristan brought his hands behind his head.

"Tristan, get the door!" Finn commanded.

Tristan froze as he saw the police.

"Tristan!" Finn yelled. "I will shoot him if you don't get the door, and the police will shoot me, so do it!"

Tristan looked at him and went to open the door for him. Finn backed into the billiards room. Tristan then closed the door. Finn pushed his father forward and the two went towards a fire exit, stepping outside to a path along the side of the house. Tristan and Mr. Cunningham walked forward with Finn behind them. They came to the back of the house and towards an open field that led to the lake.

Moored at the lakeside dock was a small sailboat. Finn led them to the boat and had them hop aboard. He then had Tristan unmoor the boat so that they could set off, heading across the lake and away from the police to another fire.

Act 6, Scene 2

Tristan looked at the summer house and how the fire had spread to the small forest around it. The fire let out a blackish smoke that joined the dark smoke in the sky above them as they went towards the forest fire. The exposed sky above was orange from the wildfire that raged on. Tristan looked towards it and saw an entire horizon that consisted of a forest ablaze.

Finn was tying his father's wrists behind his back with some rope. Afterwards, he moved away and stayed by the mast, sitting down with the gun in his lap. He avoided eye contact with Tristan and looked forward, but he kept Tristan within his peripheral vision. He had brought his mask down from his face and maintained the fabric around his neck.

"Where are we going?" Tristan questioned Finn.

"Across the water," Finn replied, "where we can be alone."

"Why the solitude? Why not just kill him now? What's the delay?"

Finn didn't reply.

Tristan shook his head and said, "You don't want to kill him now, do you? You're having second thoughts about it now that you're face-to-face with him. Before, you had adrenaline rushing through you – you were lost an in a different state of mind, and at the plant, it was a matter of escaping, but now… now it's different. You're rational self is back and he's telling you not to kill the father that raised you, or even, another human life. You're stalling."

"Shut up," Finn responded.

"Yes, how about you shut up," Mr. Cunningham agreed.

"Look at this man," Tristan went on, pointing to Cunningham at the other side of the boat, "he's not your father.

He looks nothing like you. I don't know what your mother is like, but insofar as your father, you look nothing like him."

Finn looked over to his father. Mr. Cunningham was nodding. Finn looked at him with curiosity.

"He is right," Mr. Cunningham said, "I am not your father, and neither is your mother your mother."

"What?" Finn questioned in shock.

"We adopted you when you little more than a month or two old from a foster home in France," Mr. Cunningham explained. "We took you into your lives because your mother so desperately wished to have a child, but alas, she was incapable and I was unwilling, so we adopted... I did it mostly so she would shut up. It's also the reason why you're an only child..."

"W-why didn't you ever tell me?" Finn asked. "My entire life, I've went on thinking that there was something off about me... Something inexplicably different from you and mum, and you had the answer. The two of you... that I'm not your son."

Tristan looked at Finn. He continued to maintain a state of shock in his expression as the boat continued to sail across Kielder Lake and towards the forest fire. Finn was silent.

The boat hit the shore of the opposite side of the lake. Finn stood up and motioned Tristan to go over and ashore foremost. Tristan stood up, jumped into the water and went out of the water to stand at the dirt of the beach. He felt the warmth of the forest fire hit him against the back as he stood there.

Finn turned to his adoptive-father and motioned him off the boat. Mr. Cunningham stood up and looked at the water. Finn then went to him and pushed him overboard. Mr. Cunningham struggled in the water. Finn jumped over and grabbed him. He then pushed him forward towards Tristan.

"You can't honestly believe we can go in there," Mr. Cunningham said as he looked towards the burning trees. "It's inhospitable."

"I'm not asking you to live in there, I'm asking you to die in there," Finn replied.

Mr. Cunningham turned around.

"No," Mr. Cunningham denied. "I won't go – you can kill me here, or nowhere."

Finn opened fire the rifle into the air, causing Mr. Cunningham to cower down and duck in fear. He then turned back around and went into the forest without protest. Finn pointed the gun towards Tristan. Tristan looked at him with regret and serious eyes. He followed Mr. Cunningham into the burning forest, which thankfully, did not have a lot of grass or shrubs, but consisted mainly of dirt. The forest on the opposite side of Kielder Lake from the lodge was coniferous.

In comparison to the part of the forest that Charlemagne survived through, Kielder Forest was easier to navigate and walk through even though there was a significant amount of foliage that was on fire and dangers around. There was no lack of falling debris and hazardous smoldering winds of embers.

Mr. Cunningham was particularly paranoid and careful with his steps. Unlike Finn and Tristan, he wore dress shoes that made it harder to walk, especially with his hands literally tied behind his back.

Finn had the two walk with him deep into the forest and towards a hilltop that looked down and over to the vastness of the fire. He then had Mr. Cunningham kneel down, facing the wildfire in its breadth. Finn deposited the longbow on the ground and had Tristan get rid of the arrows into the fire. Tristan was kept away and on his own as Finn walked to his adoptive-father and squatted down.

Tristan looked behind him, out towards the forest and the way he came, and then back to Finn. He gave a sigh.

"Look, Aidan," Finn said. "Look at what you've created. Look at what your greed has driven you to do."

"I see nothing wrong," Mr. Cunningham replied with a stoic face. "I made a logical choice, and many others would have done the same."

Finn shook his head and hit Mr. Cunningham in the head with the butt of his rifle.

"You know, it really is quite ironic," Tristan said with a serious face, looking to the both of them as he sat with his knees up.

"What is?" Finn questioned.

"That you don't see the hypocrisy," Tristan replied. "You hate your father because he was never there for you, I get that, but you also hate him because he participated in the act, which you told me to be evil, of destroying what is good. People are good. Nature is good. Architecture is good."

"What are you on about?" Finn then asked.

"Less than an hour ago, you set fire to your summer home, a beautiful home that was beautifully designed, and that fire spread to the trees around it that were a part of the forest (artificially separated perhaps), but still a part of the forest. You created your own little fire. You might not be this man's biological son, but you certainly act like him – you destroy. Now, you see to participate in one of the worse destructive acts, the act of murder, where one seeks to take away what God has given to us, each other. Before you object, don't forget that you were the one that told me that men are a part of nature, not apart from it. If you reject this, then you are a hypocrite to what you believe in, and all that you were talking to me what nothing more than pure rhetoric to advance your inner ambition: vengeance against your father."

"God, shut up!" Finn yelled out, standing up and going to Tristan. "You are honestly the most annoying person I had ever met! If you didn't think I'd kill you before, I might certainly do it now!"

"Do it then!" Tristan dared. "Kill me!"

Finn glared at him and then turned back to his adoptive-father. He prepared his rifle, changed its magazine, and then pointed the gun to the back of Mr. Cunningham. Mr. Cunningham lowered his head as he noticed what Finn was doing. Finn aimed the gun and held his finger over the trigger. He hesitated and Tristan could see the conflict in Finn's face as his finger froze over the trigger.

Tristan quickly stood up and brought his arms up and around Finn's shoulders so that he could pull him back as Tristan brought himself and by extension Finn, to the ground. Finn shot up and bullets launched upwards above them, going into the sky and causing some branches to let down some embers and pines.

Finn elbowed Tristan. He turned his body and punched him in the face. Tristan kicked Finn back and then attempted to tackle him to the ground. Tristan threw his own punch towards Finn, hitting him in the face. Finn grabbed Tristan by the collar and Tristan grabbed Finn by the neck.

The two struggled, and in the process of this struggle, Mr. Cunningham stood up and started to leave. Tristan noticed in the corner of his eyes and raised a fist to punch Finn. Finn's eyes wandered over to his adoptive-father as he was attempted to leave with stealth.

"Hey!" Finn shouted to him, pushing Tristan back and standing up.

Finn grabbed his rifle by the top and started to run to him. Tristan ran towards Finn as Mr. Cunningham started to run. The boys stopped as they were about to pursue one another. Mr. Cunningham brought his foot down into the soil before him at the side of the hill and earth fell down under him, causing him to stumble over and fall over.

Mr. Cunningham shouted as he fell. Finn and Tristan both looked in shock before rushing over, reaching the edge of the hill with care, and looking down and before them towards the forest fire below. He was nowhere to be seen. The fire roared as it consumed him, and Mr. Cunningham was gone.

Both of the boys continued to look down, panting from their little scrap, but eyes wide and slightly remorseful, Tristan more than Finn who appeared to be more shocked. Finn was the first to step back and walk away, turning his back on Tristan as the two stood in silence. Tristan gave the forest below another look before he turned to look at Finn. Finn held his body to the side as he looked down with a serious face. He then looked at Tristan.

The two stood apart from each other.

"Do you know what needs to happen now?" Finn questioned.

"No…" Tristan responded.

"You ruined everything," Finn replied. "You stopped me from killing the board of directors, my adoptive-father, and although I don't want to kill you, I have to. You've stood opposed to me more than anyone in my life, and I can't forgive that. I hate you. I want you dead."

Finn took the rifle in his hand, pointed it to Tristan. Tristan jumped in fright and looked shocked at Finn, but Finn unloaded the magazine and threw it aside. He also threw the rifle over and picked up the longbow. He brought it around him, attaching it to his tactical vest and holding it in place. He then looked to Tristan. Tristan looked at him.

"If either of us return out there, we'll spend life in prison, and that is a life not worth living for either of us," Finn stated. "We die here, now, and I want to die fighting you if not consumed by these flames."

Tristan raised his fists and readied himself.

"I'm not ready to die," Tristan replied, looking to him in search of mercy.

"Neither am I."

Finn ran towards Tristan. Tristan caught his hands and the two struggled, opposing forces with one another atop of the hill, hand in hand. Tristan pushed hard against Finn as he did the same with him. Tristan overcame Finn and sent him backwards onto the floor.

At the instant chance he received, Tristan ran downhill and into the forest, dodging the flames of trees and grass as he attempted to escape Finn and the certain death that waited for him. Tristan rushed through, panting and becoming lost in the maze of fire around him. Tristan shielded his face with his arms, burning them in the process before redirecting and going another direction only to be jumped by Finn.

Tristan protected himself with his burnt arms from Finn's punch. He then lowered them to look him in the face. Finn threw another punch towards him. Tristan caught his arm and pushed him back, but not before Finn threw his other arm. Tristan's head turned left as he was punched in the face. Tristan grabbed Finn's fist as it came for a second punch and attempted to pull Finn onto the ground by grabbing his elbow. Finn resisted and grabbed Tristan's left shoulder. Tristan raised his knee up in to kick Finn, but Finn lurched his body backwards.

The two spun each other so that they exchanged where they stood. They then let go of each other and raised their fists up so that they were ready to fight. Finn attempted to punch Tristan.

Tristan grabbed his arm by the elbow. Finn kicked him back. Tristan proceeded to charge back at him and tackle him onto the ground, punching Finn in the face. Finn grabbed Tristan's neck and pushed him over, exchanging places once again so that Finn was atop of him and able to punch.

Tristan's eyes widened as he saw debris from above fall towards them. He pushed Finn aside and onto the ground to his left and then rolled to right, burning his back and left lower leg in the process as it came close to a patch of fire.

The debris of wood crashed, sending embers towards Tristan. He shielded his face with his arm and felt the individual cuts and burns that gave rise. He immediately stood up and ran off from Finn next.

Tristan returned to the maze of the forest fire, rushing through and past the fires that burned in an effort to escape. He ran down a rugged path of stones and roots set aflame. He reached a very shallow rocky creek and took a moment to wipe his face with some water, albeit, warm water. He brought some to his wounds and then looked at either direction. He then looked above the ridge of the creek as Finn arrived.

Tristan continued to run as Finn jumped down, causing a splash of water as he landed in the creek. Tristan ran until he reached a portion of the ridge by the water that allowed him to climb out and return to the land. He went into the forest and navigated himself through some further flames, dodging immediate death at the hands of large fires and falling debris before reaching a cliffside that went down approximately by a story-level.

Immediately, Finn tackled Tristan down below, crashing with him to the soil. Both of them stood up and Finn went towards Tristan again. Tristan caught Finn's punch with his arm, grabbing hold of his fist before grabbing the other arm as Finn attempted to punch with it too. The two were placed in the same position they started, competing force against force. Tristan looked at Finn's eyes as it reflected the fire around and within him. Finn scowled and gritted his teeth. They broke off and grabbed one another's shoulders instead, pushing back with their foreheads an inch apart.

The two then finally pushed each other back. Tristan immediately went to punch him, and then punched him again. Finn blocked the third as he brought his arms up, but Tristan punched him in the stomach. Finn returned the punch to the stomach with one to his. He brought a fist up and gave Tristan an uppercut, bringing his fist up his chin and causing Tristan to tilt his head up. Finn then punched him in the cheek.

Tristan caught the second punch to his cheek, but Finn took his hand and then broke Tristan's grip by shaking his other hand. Afterwards, Finn grabbed Tristan's shirt by the collar and threw him down onto the ground. Tristan grabbed his wrists, but Finn broke his grip and brought his hands to Tristan's neck, grabbing his neck and holding it tightly as he choked him. Tristan brought his hands to Finn's wrists again in an attempt to get him to let go. Tristan chocked and struggled, clawing at Finn's arms as Finn held a determined face to end Tristan's life.

Tristan began to lose the will to live as he became powerless to resist Finn. He soon stopped attempting to resist and his eyes became half open. And then, it hit them. Finn was pressed atop of Tristan, breaking his grip around his neck and bringing the two close together as a flaming branch fell atop the two of them, onto Finn's back, hitting the back of his head and knocking him out. Finn being on top of Tristan broke the fall from hurting Tristan, but Tristan was now stuck with both Finn and a large tree branch atop of him.

The branch had flames that burned at Tristan's arms. He took a moment to breath, which remained difficult given the weight on his chest and lack of oxygen around, but he regained some strength as he attempted to push both Finn and the branch off together. It seemed hopeless. Tristan pushed and pushed.

He looked at Finn's unconscious face. The scar on his left cheek. His peaceful face and messy dirty blonde hair. Tristan took a deep breath and brought each hand to a side of the branch like on a barbell of a bench press. He then pushed with all his might, raising the branch up and then bringing it over his head and over the side of the hill they were on.

Tristan took an easier deep breath once the branch had been dislodged and only Finn's mass was atop of him, still unconscious. Tristan wrapped his arms around Finn and gently brought him onto his back before he could stand up. Tristan then knelt over him and brought his face over his mouth.

The airway was clear. He was breathing and given the heated atmosphere around them, he was warm but showing no signs of shock. Tristan took another deep breath and sat back with his knees up in front of him. He wiped the sweat over his forehead and let out a deep exhale.

Act 6, Scene 3

Tristan stood up and looked around him. The fire was more intense in the part below the cliff he had been pushed down as the trees and bushes were more densely packed together. Tristan went to Finn and attempted to wake him by pushing at his body.

"Finn!" Tristan yelled. "Finn!"

Finn was unresponsive to his voice. Tristan applied a bit of pain to Finn's thumb. He kicked his leg, but didn't awaken. Tristan took the longbow off of Finn and brought it around his own back to carry.

"Wake up, you idiot!" Tristan pleaded, pushing at him to wake.

Tristan sighed and looked around him again, this time eyeing a pathway out of where they were. He looked at Finn and took his arm, raising his torso up and bringing his own shoulder into Finn's body so that it could rest on him. He then pulled with all his strength in an attempt to rest Finn onto his shoulder, but it failed. Finn fell back and Tristan let out a pant as he sat down.

"Come on... he can't weight much," Tristan said to himself, looking at Finn's unconscious body. "I've had over two-hundred pounds rest on my shoulder when doing squats. I can carry a person..."

Tristan went to Finn again and took his arm. Finn's knees were bent. He raised Finn up and got him to stand. Tristan then bent over, bringing Finn's body over his and Finn's arm that he had over his shoulder. Tristan grabbed Finn's leg and raised him over, bringing the arm to the same hand whose arm was ahold of Finn's thigh so that he had a free arm.

With Finn in his grip, he started to make his way out of the forest at a slower pace. Tristan struggled to keep Finn on his back as went along, keeping away from flames and fire as he tried to navigate a way out. He looked up to the sky above for direction, but there was nothing but thick grey clouds of smoke. He went along but stopped as some debris blocked his path. He took a step back and went another direction.

Tristan stopped in the middle of his tracks, slightly squatting and pulling Finn's body back up before continuing along. He met another dead-end and proceeded to navigate around the edge for an opening until he found himself going back the way he came. Tristan stopped and looked around. He decided to go back the way he came and restart, going the other direction.

Finn continued to sleep as he rested on Tristan's shoulders. Tristan passed a clearing and came into a part of the forest with little shrubs. He was able to effectively navigate himself through until he reached a ridge. Tristan looked at the ridge and foot drop he had to make before he looked at the water.

The water and stream looked familiar to the one he had crossed earlier and that Finn was chasing him down. Tristan looked up and down at the sides of the creek. He took a step back and retraced his steps, returning into the part of the forest with more shrubs. He came to a cliffside similar to the one that Finn had pushed him down and followed it until the land smoothed out for him to easily go down.

Tristan continued along, struggling to carry Finn and producing large streaks of sweat along his face. Tristan's hair was wet with his own sweat and appeared as if he had been swimming. He kept ahold of Finn and stopped as he met the dead-end of a trail he had been following. All around him with the exception of where he came was covered with some fiery barrier that prevented him from going forward. Tristan looked around with an exhausted face, brought a knee down and gently lowered Finn onto the ground.

Afterwards, he sat down and brought his body back to rest on Finn's. Tristan panted and held a tired and painful face. He wiped at the sweat on his face, but his arms had become so wet that he was unable to properly dry himself. He looked uncomfortable for this. Tristan stood up and looked around. He looked back the way he came and then up.

"Help!" Tristan shouted. "I need help! Anybody – if you can hear me – help!"

Tristan then looked down and over to Finn. He walked over and brought a knee down next to him and kept a hand over his body. He re-assessed his airway to see if it was clear, bringing his face to Finn's mouth to check for breathing as well and then moving his face back so that he could bring a hand to his cheek and check for temperature. Unlike Tristan, Finn's face was dry and in a better shape than Tristan's who had cuts and burns. Tristan took some deep breaths, which were gasped due to the limited oxygen around. He then looked to Finn. He closed his eyes with pain, clenching his eye lids tightly closed before opening them. He then pushed Finn onto his back and took his hands to open Finn's mouth.

The fire crackled around them and Tristan took some deep breaths. Tristan breathed in with the gasps of air that he attempted to keep in his mouth, concentrating what little oxygen there was into Finn's mouth to give him life. He did this once and then moved his head away to take his own breaths. Once he felt sufficient, he closed in to give Finn some more oxygen.

Finn began to move around as if he was waking up in bed from a deep sleep. Tristan gave off his last breath and moved his face and head away. Finn woke up and looked around. He brought a hand to his face and rubbed around before looking to Tristan.

"W-what happened?" Finn questioned.

"A branch fell on us while you were trying to kill me," Tristan replied. "I got us out, but we're now stuck here."

Finn looked around and saw the mess they were in. He sat up and breathed.

"Take it easy…" Tristan warned, bringing a hand to Finn's shoulder. "We need to get out of here as soon as possible, otherwise we're going to pass out because of the lack of oxygen or worse, because of carbon monoxide."

Finn nodded and stood up with Tristan's help. He looked around and started to remove the top layer of his tactical suit, throwing the jacket to the ground and exposing his tank top underneath. He then brought a hand through his hair and held a compass in his hand.

"Kielder Lake is in the south – this way is north," Finn said, pointing towards the direction they came. "Sucks, but we're going to have to go back and then out."

"Okay," Tristan replied. "Let's go then."

The two set off and went backwards along a trail before reaching a part of the forest fire where they had more liberty in their sense of direction. Finn led them west and they went along, attempting to go south. Finn navigated and led the way through the forest with his compass, reaching through tight spaces and crawling beneath fallen debris that still burned as they passed by.

The boys covered themselves from falling debris and within a couple of minutes, they reached a hilltop in the distance. The two travelled eastward and then came to an uphill portion of land that reached a smooth plateau for them to continue travelling forward.

At the end of the plateau was a long canyon that stretched out at either direction and was side. Below the canyon were some trees and bushes creating a similar hellish display as that which consumed Mr. Cunningham.

Tristan and Finn looked around the edges of the cliffside of the canyon for a path around, but it seemed as though none existed.

"There had to be another way," Tristan said, looking to Finn.

Finn shook his head.

"It's here or nowhere," Finn replied. "Like you said, we can spend time backtracking in an attempt to get a better deal, risk dying of lack of oxygen or because of CO, or we can take what we have and attempt to cross. Come on, help me push this log over and we can bridge past."

Finn went to the trunk of a burnt tree and started to attempt to push it over. The trunk was long enough to extend the entire width of the canyon (approximately seven-eight meters). Tristan went over and tried to help Finn push the trunk. The two pushed against the tree with all their force, causing the burnt trunk to snap and tip over, landing on the opposite side without snapping in half.

"You go first," Finn offered. "I'll follow."

"Okay," Tristan replied, climbing atop of the burnt log and starting to carefully go along the narrow path ahead.

Once Tristan was a meter forward, Finn climbed up and followed. The two crossed the trunk as though it were a gymnastic beam, bringing their arms out to maintain balance. Tristan brought his foot down and felt it slip. He quickly reaffirmed his grip and continued forward. He was almost past.

Behind him, Finn kept his head down to watch his feet. He went along with careful steps, looking up to look at Tristan from behind before looking down quickly as his own foot slipped. Tristan heard Finn lose his balance. Finn fell over and grabbed the trunk with his arms. He was able to hold on, but the violent nature of the fall caused the trunk to shake and Tristan to fall on his bottom with his legs apart. He held on to the trunk with his arms and looked back to Finn.

"Tristan!" Finn shouted to him. "Help!"

"I'm coming," Tristan replied, crawling back towards Finn, keeping his stomach pressed against the trunk and reaching him. "Grab my hand!"

Finn grabbed Tristan's hand. Finn attempted to pull himself up while Tristan tried to pull at him with what strength the two of them had left.

"Ow!" Finn shouted, losing grip with his other hand.

Tristan was pulled forward slightly as Finn fell down. Tristan held on to the trunk with his other hand and legs, keeping Finn suspended in the air as he held on to Tristan by their hands.

"Hold on!" Tristan encouraged. "I can pull you back up."

Finn looked down at the hellfire below with scared eyes. He then looked over to Tristan. Tristan looked at him and saw a glimmer of a tear in the corner of his eye. He looked apologetic.

"Don't let go," Tristan said in a calm voice, struggling to hold on. "Please don't let go…"

Tristan's eyes began to water.

"Please…" Tristan begged.

"If I make it out with you, all I have to look forward to is prison for the rest of my life…" Finn confessed. "I can't do that… even for my best friend."

"Shut up!" Tristan responded. "You idiot! You're not my best friend! You're more than that! You're my brother!"

Finn gave a light shrewd smile at him. He shook his head.

"I'm sorry for trying to kill you, but I have to let go, otherwise you'll lose your strength and we'll both die," Finn said to him. "For that… I'm sorry too."

Finn let go of Tristan's hand and Tristan watched with tearful eyes as Finn plummeted to his demise.

"No!" Tristan shouted with a broken voice. "No! Finn! No!" Tristan couldn't see him. The smoke arising from below was too much for him to see what was past the trees and before him. He lay atop of the trunk, hugging it as he cried and maintained one hand embracing the trunk and the other relaxed, drooped down in defeat. Tristan cried with a great amount of pain at the loss of his brotherly friend.

Once he had composed himself, he pushed his weak body against the trunk and carefully turned back around to continue along the rest of the path. Once there, he stood up on weak feet and looked behind in an attempt to see if he could see Finn. He couldn't.

Past the trees was too much smoke for him to make out where he was. He took a step back and looked towards the forest. His body was trembling. He took a step away and slowly walked onwards.

Tristan was lifeless, but at the same time, there was some sort of invisible glow around him that made him impervious to the dangers around – he was careless. Tristan marched his way through the rest of the forest and came to the end, reaching the beaches of the lake at a grass field beforehand. He took his first steps over the field and then collapsed to the ground. He was not unconscious. He crawled forward, digging his hands into the dirt until he couldn't go any further. Tristan looked at the dirt in his hand.

The dirt was dark brown, had a moist texture and was soft. Tristan looked at the blades of grass atop and the roots below, implanted into the field around. He let go of the dirt and brought his head down to the side. He lay down on the field, still conscious, but virtually paralyzed. He stayed like this for what seemed like minutes upon minutes until he felt the vibration of footsteps rush towards him.

Tristan closed his eyes, but felt his body turned onto his back. He then felt a mask come over his mouth and nose. He fell unconscious with his eyes looking upwards to the trees past the rescue workers around him, looking at the patches of blue sky through the grey clouds until he was definitely asleep.

Epilogue

Tristan lay atop of the bed in his room in a hospital in Edinburgh. His hair had been shaved due to a wound on his head that required sutures. In addition, his arms were covered in gauze from the burns he experienced and his right shoulder was wrapped in bandage, but in sum, Tristan looked cleaner than when he was in the forest. His skin was dry, tanned, and he was dressed in a light blue hospital gown. He had a nasal cannula up his nostrils, or pair of tubes, providing oxygen and the bed was raised for him to sit up as he looked at the TV across from him. On his left arm was an intravenous needle hooked up to an IV pole with a bag of white liquid going into his veins and at his index finger of his right hand was a probe, or pulse oximeter monitoring his oxygen levels and pulse.

The bedroom he was in was tight and only had the one bed. There were various childish designs as the room was part of a pediatric ward. On his left was a window that looked out to the Scottish city and in front to the left was a door that went into the bathroom. The windows could be opened to let in air, but they had been closed as an air conditioner was running. Currently, it was dark outside and a clock in front of the bed said that it was a couple minutes past nine o'clock.

Tristan looked defeated and emotionless as he lay in bed, looking at the TV without focus. He appeared to be lost and depressed. His attention diverted as he heard a knock on the door to his right. Tristan looked over and saw Diana there with some balloons and Charlemagne with her. The two stepped inside. Tristan could see Miklos and Lukas behind, dressed in suits.

"Hey," Diana said, going over to him and hugging him.

"Ow," Tristan complained as Diana brought her arms around Tristan's back.

"Sorry…" Diana responded, letting go and looking to him as she held the balloons. "I haven't seen you in so long… I've missed you."

"I've missed you too," Tristan replied in a raspy voice, giving a shy smile to her.

Tristan then looked to Charlemagne who stood apart from them, observing before stepping forward.

"Sorry it took so long for us to visit, but I had a hard time searching every hospital in the United Kingdom for a boy recovered at Kielder Water," Charlemagne stated. "Not that it mattered in the end, because the head warden told me where you were… You had no form of identification on you, so I suppose searching for you proved useless, but nonetheless. I'm glad you're alive – it has never been a better birthday present, I suppose."

"Happy Birthday, Charles," Tristan replied. "I'm sorry you spent it like this, and now here."

"Nonsense," Charlemagne said. "My birthday means little to me at this age."

"Here," Diana then said, handing him the balloons. "I got you these before we came."

"Thanks… they're cute," Tristan replied, taking them. "Can you do me a favor? Can you get me some water, please?"

"Yeah, of course," Diana replied, taking a step back. "I'll be right back."

Diana left and once she left, Tristan looked to Charlemagne.

"I'm sorry," Tristan confessed, eyes tearing. "I'm sorry for everything… for going behind your back, for…"

"Hey…" Charlemagne said, bringing a hand to his shoulder to settle him. "Stop."

Tristan's heart rate elevated on the monitor.

"I couldn't save him… I- he's dead, and…"

Charlemagne looked back at him with stunned eyes. He turned his head to the side.

"I couldn't save your son," Tristan said. "I- I'm sorry."

"You have nothing to apologize for," Charlemagne replied with a saddened look.

"Finn was your son."

"You are my son too."

Charlemagne took a moment. Tristan wiped his eyes with his arm. Diana returned with the water and handed it to Tristan. Tristan took it without giving thanks and looked out the window.

"So..." Diana said, "when you do think you'll be getting out."

"I'm not sure," Tristan replied. "For a start, I'm on antibiotics in case of infections," he said, pulling at the tube attached to his IV, "and they couldn't really release me until Charles showed up or else they would have phoned the Canadian Embassy, but now that he's here, it's just a matter of getting discharged by the doctor tomorrow morning, I guess. If there's nothing... physically wrong with me. You know, in case I don't have any sort of infectious disease."

"I'll be sure to be here for that," Charlemagne replied. "Both of us."

Tristan looked to the TV as it displayed the BBC News. The volume was silent but showed footage of what had happened two days ago. Tristan read the closed captions.

"Cunningham Industries is being investigated by the Department of Environment, Farmland, and Rural Affairs in relation to the forest fire..." Charlemagne said. "According to the work of some clever scientists, their activities were responsible for what occurred. This, tied in with Mr. Cunningham's disappearance presumed death, has sent stock prices for Cunningham Industries to crash."

Tristan gave a brief smile. His face then rested down.

"Yeah," Tristan simply said in response.

Diana looked to Tristan with concern. She brought a hand to his. He deflected it.

"Is everything okay?" Diana questioned.

"Yeah," Tristan replied. "I'm just a little tired."

Diana looked at him with doubt.

"In better news," Charlemagne went on, "I've talked with my sister and she's going to work with the ministry to commit the foundation to assist with the restoration of the lands that were affected so that they may have a speedy recovery. Her hopes are to turn a certain portion of the lands into a wildlife reserve where certain species that were lost to the British Isle can be reintroduced in an artificial ecosystem."

"Not artificial," Tristan responded. "Just because man made the ecosystem that way, doesn't mean it's artificial... man is a part of nature."

Charlemagne looked to Tristan strangely.

"Yes," Charlemagne replied. "I suppose that is true."

Diana looked at Tristan with concern.

"Anyways," Charlemagne said with a sigh, "it was nice to see you, but perhaps it's time Diana and I left to get some rest. We've had a hectic day and they won't let us stay with you, I'm afraid as visiting hours are to eight o'clock.

"Come along, Diana," Charlemagne encouraged.

Diana looked to Tristan as she left. She continued to hold a look of concern on her face as the two separated. Tristan didn't look to her and instead looked across his room and to the ground. Once they were gone, his face dropped to a frown. He continued to lie in bed for a couple of minutes until he pushed back at his covers and got out of bed.

Tristan walked over and closed the door to his room, pulling at the IV pole to follow him before he went back around and towards the window. Tristan pulled the window open, but it only went so far to prevent people from jumping out. Once the window was open, Tristan sat down on the ledge and looked out to the city of Edinburgh.

The city had a mixture of traditional architecture in the form of brownstone apartments and cobblestone streets. A tower in the distance had a clock with a bright yellow light like the bell tower of Westminster Palace. There were additional towers with spires scattered and beyond, atop of the hill, was some sort of castle.

Tristan looked at all of that and then up to the cloudless night skies. There weren't as many stars in the city as there were in the forest. Tristan looked at the sky with slight disappointment before eyeing the slightly full moon. He focused on the moon and tilted his head back. A tear fell down Tristan's left eye and he proceeded to howl, pressing his lips forward and yowling out a saddened howl.

"And the Lord took the man, and put him in the Garden of Eden to dress it and to keep it. And the Lord commanded to the man, saying, Of every tree of the garden you may freely eat: But of the tree of knowledge of good and evil, you shall not eat of it: for in the day that you eat thereof you shall surely die."

– Genesis 2:15-17

www.ingramcontent.com/pod-product-compliance
Lightning Source LLC
Chambersburg PA
CBHW051433170626
46809CB00006B/2445